TIGER DICK'S DOUBLOONS

**BOOKS IN THE ARGOSY LIBRARY:**

# TIGER DICK'S DOUBLOONS

## DON MCGREW

ILLUSTRATED BY
## JOHN R. NEILL

COVER BY
## PAUL STAHR

POPULAR PUBLICATIONS · 2025

# TIGER DICK'S DOUBLOONS

*In the days when full-rigged ships sailed
the Spanish Main, young Ned Allen
set sail for the American colonies—and
for as strange adventures as ever man
met in those buccaneering times*

# 1

## THE INN OF FEAR

**IT WAS IN** the year of 1775 that I finished my education in England, just in time to receive word that my father's Virginia estates had been confiscated by the colonial authorities because of his activities in the Sons of Liberty.

That was the reason for my presence on the Liverpool water front, with only a few shillings remaining in my possession; for I was looking for a chance to work my passage homeward. It likewise accounted for my temporary abiding place in a little room under the gables of Jed Morgan's "Sign of the Anchor"—from the tiny window of which I could see Liverpool's horrid gibbets, stark against the evening sky; and it brought about my acquaintance with the huge, burly innkeeper, who lived in such deadly fear of "a seagoing chap with a silvery whistle."

My landlord, Jed Morgan, had a visage to frighten a child into spasms at candlelight, and his bulk was tremendous.

I had seen him crack the heads of two hardy seamen between his hamlike palms as easily as you or I might have handled little children. Scarred, he was, and forbidding; a leathery man with bared forearms the thickness of ship's spars, and a truculent, battered countenance, frightful to behold. Yet I had spent but little time within the place when I discovered that this formidable giant was afraid of some one!

This truth became more and more apparent to me as the days passed. He never came over to your table without first looking toward the door; and once, when a naval officer ran in hurriedly to announce an accident across the way, Jed whirled like a flash and almost pinned the stranger to the wall.

Quicker than most men could wink he had produced a heavy, ugly knife; and there he stood, as white as chalk, with the knife aloft in his great hand, while the stranger stared at him with bulging eyes and dropped jaw.

Then Jed recovered himself, and the color returned to his heavy face in a wave. If ever a man looked foolish, it was Jed. He gave the roomful a surly glance, spat upon the floor, and stumped away to his back room.

Sitting at my table in the taproom at the time was an old, wind-roughened tar. He was an habitue of the place, who had told me he was looking for a berth at sea.

Tom Newgate was his name, and though Jed was the last man in the world to pose as a jovial landlord—seeming to have no intimates, and being downright surly with his customers—it appeared that he and Tom had been ship-mates on some cruise or other, and Jed would occasionally call the old fellow into his private room.

**HAVING STRUCK UP** an acquaintance with the mild old seaman, I seized this chance to question him about our host.

"What," I demanded, "do you make of that?"

Old Newgate was past sixty, and wise with the ways of men ashore and afloat. His eyes twinkled and nearly

*Jed sprang at the luckless officer*

disappeared in nutbrown wrinkles. He lifted a tar-stained hand with black, broken nails to a broad, stubby nose, and worked his ale glass around in circles with the other.

"Son," said he, staring into the ale, "maybe you think that man Jed is rough—and you ain't guessed wrong, not you. But there's men afloat as would make chicken meat o' Jed, and you may lay to it."

"They must be monsters, then!" I cried.

"Well, I has one in mind as is suthin' to keep a body awake o' nights," he said, rolling his quid.

"You mean the one that Jed's afraid of?"

"Now, how would I know?" the old fellow cried quickly, glancing about. Then he chuckled. "It's kind of funny, though," he confided. "I mean Jed bein' afraid. P'tickly when I thinks of what a sweet singin' angel Jed was hisself, at sea."

"It seems ridiculous for him to remain here as landlord of a public house if he's afraid of being found," I declared.

"That's the cream o' the joke, Mr. Allen. An old uncle left this to Jed. Jed, he's got the first sov'ring he ever earned.

He could no more sell this here grog shop below a proper figger than you could twist your own mother's neck. At the same time he's atween the devil and the deep sea for fear this man will heave to in the offing afore he can sell the place."

"What sort of man does he fear?" I eagerly inquired, conjuring up the picture of a gorilla in human form.

"Son," said Newgate, "how would I know? Jed don't let his jaw tackle slip much, as you may have noticed. You might arsk him yourself, though." And he grinned.

This by no means appealed to me. I was nearly six feet in height, but my head barely rose above Jed's shoulder. So for a time I was forced to content myself with conjectures in which Jed's scars conjured up pictures of blood-smeared decks and cutlasses clashing in terrific struggles for the prize within the hold.

Old Tom said that he had made but one cruise with the man, on a peaceful merchantman, but while Tom was not one you would have pictured as a pirate, it was easy enough to visualize Jed with a leg thrown over the bulwarks and a cutlass gripped between his powerful teeth. It was my guess that he had tricked some former messmate in the division of loot.

It was not until a week later that Jed finally called me aside on his own initiative and threw light upon the matter. The old guests had by then departed, and Tom had secured a berth aboard the *Bonny Lee,* then riding at anchor in the harbor and taking cargo aboard for Charleston.

I had tried to get a berth on this same *Bonny Lee,* only to be told that the crew was made up; and that same day I had told Jed that I must give up my lodgings because my funds were almost gone.

"Son," said he, lowering his voice to a husky, croaking pitch and looking round to be sure that no one overheard, "I thinks I knows a gentleman when I sees one. Now, you ain't had no luck shipping out, and within the week I expects to sell this here grog shop, lock, stock and barrel. I'm going to sail with old Tom on the *Bonny Lee* for the colonies, I am. You're a wanting food and lodging and a billet home, says you. Says I to you, 'I'm a needin' a little help. Suppose we trade?'"

There was an anxious, worried look which he could not keep from the depths of his shrewd, piglike eyes. Noting this, I said, a bit sharply, "That's according to the nature of the trade."

"Why, it's nothing that need worrit you, my hearty!" he hastened to assure me. "Ah, but I knows the ways of gentlemen, I does."

"All right, then," said I. "Let's have it."

**THE PERSPIRATION SUDDENLY** stood out in great drops on his wrinkled, low forehead, and he seemed ashamed to meet my glance. At last he looked up with a half aggressive, half apologetic air, met my eye for an instant, and turned his head away. He seemed to be centering his vision upon some horrid memory of the past.

"I ain't no coward!" he croaked. "I ain't a feared o' storm at sea, nor any ten swabs as ever trod a deck. Not me, Mr. Allen. I've seen them as shook at thought of a gibbet, and them as was a-scared to lean too far over the lee rail, because o' sharks; but I never seed the day I give a fig for man nor devil till—till this came on me."

He shuddered here, like a woman. "I'll own up square," he cried. "I'm squeamish o' snakes. Maybe that's why, 'cause he's got snake's blood in his veins, that I'm a feared o' this fellow Tiger Dick."

"The man you're watching for!" slipped from me.

"The same," he assented, more easily. He wiped his brow. "You've noticed; you ain't no fool, not you. Well, all you got to do is to help watch for him, d'y'see? You do that, and you'll have food and lodging, Mr. Allen, till such time as you puts your foot aboard a proper ship."

I thought it over a moment, and saw nothing in the transaction to trouble my conscience. "I'll do it," I agreed. "Only, what manner of man am I to watch for?"

"Thankee, sir!" he cried, in great relief. "And what manner o' man is he, says you? Why, he's a large, redfaced, black-eyed man, as large as me, is Tiger Dick. A man as could pass for a jolly chapling, or a hearty, honest squire, a handin' round juicy chunks o' beef to his tenants at a Candlemas barbecue. Ay, that's the man. Ten to one he'll be a whistlin', he will, so sweet as any mocking bird. Mind that. So sweet as any mocking bird."

"That's not much to go on," I said.

"Ah, but it is, sir. You never heard a whistle like it, and never will again. You'll not mistake him for a landsman, either. Nor that ain't all. I expects you'll see a seafarin' dwarf with him. A little, ugly dwarf."

Again Jed shuddered, and spat. "That dwarf is an ugly, twisted, snarling brute," he added. "So pleasant-lookin' as a black cloud heavin' up 'twixt ship and the home shore. Bruno is what Tiger Dick calls him, and they're seldom apart."

A few more details of description were given me, and I took up sentry duty on a chair just outside the door. Jed was in deadly fear that Tiger Dick might arrive while he—Jed—was "below decks," as he put it, tapping a new cask. In this case I was to stamp heavily—three times—upon the taproom floor.

**FOR FIVE DAYS** nothing happened, and as the hours wore away toward noon observation of the sixth it appeared that Jed had suffered his alarms for nothing, and that he would be standing safely out to sea before sundown that afternoon. The *Bonny Lee* was scheduled to sail with the evening tide.

It was just after lunch, as I remember well, of a fine, clear, cheery day, with the white clouds drifting by in a blue sky, and the quays alive with noisy trucks and drays, and the harbor a forest of tall masts that tapered to needle points, when I sighted the large, jovial seaman, with the gnarled dwarf trotting behind him, like a dog, two paces in his rear.

Jed was expecting the prospective purchaser of the inn at any moment, but had gone below to broach a cask. Tom Newgate had come ashore from the *Bonny Lee* for some duffle and was sitting in the taproom at the time, with half a dozen tarred seamen lolling near.

What with watching the longshoremen handling high piles of bales and barrels on the wharves, and giving half an ear to the lusty chant of open-breasted seamen who were pulling on a rope aboard the distant *Bonny Lee*, I was not on the *qui vive*, and not immediately certain of Tiger Dick's identity.

The strange pair came quickly around the end of a dray, some distance off. The large man was not whistling. Then

I saw them more clearly, and noted that both wore sailors' garb. My heart began to pound. They came a few steps nearer; and suddenly I arose, and whipped inside. With thunderous impact I brought my heel down three times upon the floor.

The half dozen sailors at the tables looked up with round eyes. Then something crashed below, and Jed came rushing up the stairs. His face was a mask of sickly white under his tan as he burst through the door, knife upraised.

"Where?" he gasped. "Where?"

He was too far back in the room to have my point of vantage, but I nodded toward the window through which I could see the dreaded pair approaching. As for myself, I was chiefly conscious of amazement.

The dwarf, Bruno, was indeed more repulsive than an ape. He swung along on crooked, oddly bent legs, his great, powerful, hairy hands dangling gorilla-like close to the walk. At each ungainly, rolling step he peered pugnaciously here and there from red-rimmed, ferocious eyes. These were overshadowed by coarse, black brows; his horrid face and body were fairly matted with thick, black hair; and the contrast he afforded to his master struck me as tragically absurd.

"Something," I thought, "must have addled poor Jed's pate a bit."

Never had I looked upon a more pleasant man than this great, neat, round-faced seaman in his trig suit of stout blue sea cloth, who carried his bulk with such a light and jaunty step. His round, full face was smooth, and fat, and very red, with a double chin; his wig was white as snow; and to add another touch of contrast to his color scheme, his large eyes were black and soft as liquid. When he looked down at Bruno and revealed his teeth in a radiant smile, it warmed my heart.

It was the dwarf that Jed should have feared, I thought. As for the big seaman—who appeared to be about forty years of age—I would have been inclined to trust him anywhere.

Jed, on the other hand, quivered in such terror as one is loath to look upon.

Then as the pair came opposite the window, Tiger Dick suddenly threw back his head and began to whistle.

Whether it was at the third bar or the fourth I do not recall; but as I stood there, expecting I knew not what in the way of violence on the part of Jed, there was a crash behind me. I wheeled, and saw that Jed had fallen full length upon the floor.

# 2

## THE MAN WHO WHISTLED

**THERE WAS A** second or so of stunned silence in the
taproom, before Tiger Dick appeared in the open doorway.
He paused abruptly, and broke short off in his whistling.
He was staring at the recumbent figure upon the sanded
planks with a look of amazement.

At the same moment old Newgate and two others
hurriedly moved to pick up the fallen man, while Bruno,
the dwarf, began plucking at Dick's sleeve with one hand
and pointing excitedly at Jed with the other. Meanwhile
he chattered unintelligibly in a horrid jargon, and I sickened at sight of his mouth. His tongue had been cut out.

"Why, bless my soul, if it ain't my old shipmate, Jed!"
Dick exclaimed, in a wondrously melodious voice. "Old
Jed, as ever was. There, there, Bruno, be still; I understand.
And old Tom Newgate! Well, shiver my sides, but this
here's a happenstance. I didn't know that you came ashore,
Tom. And what the devil's wrong with Jed, might I ask?"

Tom lowered Jed to a seat on a chair, and reached diffi-
dently for his forelock. "Why, Mr. Buntline, it seems like
he went and fainted when he heard you whistle, sir."

Dick was the picture of incredulity. "Now, fancy that!"

he gasped. He inverted both thumbs and pointed at his breast. "You mean old Jed was afeared o' *me?*"

The man was pursy, so to speak, from good living, and appeared so good-natured and mild, and looked round at us with so comical an air that I could not help but chuckle. Whereupon he broke into laughter on his own account. It was laughter that doubled him over, caught up the whole assemblage with its contagion, and ended with him gasping for breath upon a chair.

"That roaring old typhoon afeared o' *me!*" he gasped. "I never heared the beat." But a second later found him sobering. "Are you sure he was right aloft, Tom?"

Before Tom could answer, another man removed his hand from Jed's breast.

"Why, see here!" the fellow cried. "Jed ain't fainted. He's on the long shore."

"He is, and no mistake!" breathed Tom Newgate, crossing himself.

I saw at a glance that this was true: the color had drained from Jed's blue face, and the mouth gaped slackly in death. Fright had paralyzed his rum-soaked heart.

Dick stood stock-still for a second or two, his mouth agape. Then he moved toward the dead man. I had never seen a big man move so quickly and so noiselessly.

"He's gone to his last home, sure enough!" he exclaimed in a shocked voice. Hurriedly he crossed himself and looked round at us, his round face concerned. "Now, lookee here, gentlemen," he cried. "You've heard Tom Newgate say as how Jed here was afeared o' me. This here is a rum go for me, this is. But you'll bear witness, one and all, that

I was never so much as in the room when poor Jed dived hatches under—won't you, now?"

"I could, but I think it's our cue to budge, mates, afore the coroner puts his oar in," returned a tall, sallowfaced seaman, moving uneasily toward the door. "You know how these courts are. Well, then, this here ain't no affair o' mine; leastwise I can't nowise see it that way; so I'm for the open air, mates."

"Me, too," said another; and all save Tom Newgate, the frightened boy-of-all-work, and myself made themselves scarce, leaving Dick and the silent dwarf to face their dilemma.

One knowing the circumstances could hardly blame them. Although there was no wound of any sort upon Jed's slack body, the stolid British authorities had a way of holding witnesses incommunicado until they were certain that "there was no bottom to come at."

**I SAW MYSELF** being held with the rest, my circumstances inquired into, and the possibility of impressment aboard a British ship as an unemployed colonial subject without means of support; and I was on the point of following, when Tiger Dick Buntline spoke up.

"I saw you jump back inside the door," said he. "Come now, was you a warning of Jed?"

"Why, yes," I replied, seeing no reason for quibbling.

"And why?" he wanted to know.

I told him, briefly enough, of my strange compact with Jed, and the reasons for it.

"Crazy he must have been, plain crazy!" sighed Dick, wiping his brow with a silk handkerchief. "Here, though: this ain't shipshape, this ain't. You, boy," addressing the stupid yokel whom Jed had employed about the place, you hop it for the coroner, double quick. Here's a golden sov'ring for your trouble, my lad."

The boy was off on the run, and immediately Dick turned and seized my lapel between thumb and forefinger.

"Mate," he said pleadingly, while the sweat stood out on his brow, "here's a fine lay for an innocent man, now ain't it? There goes that boy with next to my last sov'ring, so help me. Here's a mate sick on the *Bonny Lee,* bound out on the tide this very afternoon as ever was for Charleston—and me signed up to take that mate's berth. Through a tip from Tom, here, this very noon. Now, if that ain't tough, then scuttle me. Hey, Tom?"

"Tough?" said Tom. "I reckon it's tough, sir. Tough ain't no name for it."

It was all confusing to me. I could not reconcile Jed's fears with my impression of Tiger Dick; the name, it seemed to me, must have been given by way of a joke; and Dick read my face easily enough and profited by it.

"We're in a clove hitch, we two," he declared. "We three, in fact. You know how they'll hold you for a witness. If you tell that story to a coroner, why, like as not, they'll hold me a year till they can get—well, the Lord knows what they'll do. Suppose, now, we budge. Tom was telling me of you this very noon, as ever was. Suppose I gets you a berth aboard the *Bonny Lee?*"

I hesitated. Something warned me, but the voice was very faint. Why, I asked myself, was I in any way obligated to languish in a cell till the highhanded, muddling authorities concluded their red-tape investigations? Moreover, the man had done nothing in my presence to merit the loss of his billet.

"Don't hang in stays, Mr. Allen!" urged Dick. "Time's passing."

"Are you sure you can place me aboard?" I returned. "I tried that vessel this week, and Captain Fogg—that is correct, isn't it?—told me he was full up."

"If that's all that's bothering you," said Dick, linking his arm in mine and urging me toward the door, "let's go. Supercargo is wot I have in mind, my lad. You're an educated gentleman; I seed that the minute I laid eyes on you. Looking for a supercargo was what I came down street for. What luck! Lord strike me pink, but here we go, four good colonials"—here he lowered his voice—"and to hell with his majesty and all his tax collectors, is what I say."

"Amen to that!" I echoed fervently.

So that's how I shipped aboard the *Bonny Lee*, and got clear away with the tide that same afternoon without having sighted a bailiff or learning what befell when the gawping boy of-all-work returned with the coroner. It was a great relief to me when I heard our tar-stained, weather-beaten salts tramping round the capstan with Dick singing:

> "Yo ho ho! A sailing go we—
> Yo ho ho! For the High Barbaree,
> As jolly a lot of tars, lads, as ever put to sea!"

At each final "ho!" the men sang out in unison and shoved the bars before them. Not long afterward the anchor was up snug, and we were going about and about between the buoys, with the gruesome gibbets growing smaller and smaller in our eyes as we left them astern, and our bows treading musically upon the waters as we headed for the blue and smiling sea. Dangerous as sea voyages are apt to be, I watched with delighted eyes the foaming combers spreading away from our prow, and inhaled deeply, enjoying to the full the tang of the salt air. Little did I dream that I was to encounter, not only storm at sea, but adventures that were to shape the course of my whole life.

# 3

## A BLACK SHIP OF WAR

**FOR A TIME** there was no incident in that outward voyage worth recording. The *Bonny Lee* was a trig and well-founded Yankee schooner, beautifully rigged alow and aloft, and painted in reds and whites. Ah, but there was a combination of beauty and seaworthiness!

She had been built in Boston, sat the water like a swan, and carried a heavy, miscellaneous cargo without materially lessening her speed. A breath would set her moving, and every man in a contented crew was in love with her.

Cap'n Fogg was a worthy commander of that bonny craft, too. He was a spare, stern Yankee, somewhere in his late forties, and an incisive man when giving a command; but he was just and fair, and not at all niggardly with his duff. As we skimmed along under full sail, it seemed that we were destined to make Charleston after as fine a voyage as ever was made by a happy and competent crew.

A riffle did appear one day upon our serene horizon, of which I must make mention. Engaged at the last hour, as I was, to replace a supercargo who disappeared ashore, I labored for a time under the impression that our cargo was correctly described in the manifest. This listed everything from plows to rolls of silk.

To all intents and purposes the *Bonny Lee* was bent on delivering to the troublesome colonies nothing but legitimate articles, for peaceful usage. Nor did I discover my error until, being in the hold when some boxes marked "Plowshares" were being moved for better storage, one of them was accidentally dropped. I saw then that the broken box contained muskets!

"Might 've known something like that would happen!" grunted Cap'n Fogg. "Well, so be it." He took me aside. "Now that you know they're aboard, my lad," said he, "I'll tell you they're for the Sons of Liberty. I don't go in for smuggling, as a rule, but this is different."

"You can count on me for silence, sir!" I assured him fervently—for I would have helped any one, at any risk, to smuggle contraband in the name of liberty.

"I'm sure of that," said he. "As for the crew, they're not all good colonials. But"—here he looked at me shrewdly—"I reckon that a few pounds among 'em will put their tongues in their cheeks."

This discovery gave me cause for worry, now and again; for whenever a strange sail appeared on the horizon, I wondered if we were to be overhauled by a British man-o'-war. Yet this was only at first. As Tiger Dick pointed out, the *Bonny Lee* could show a clean pair of heels to any man-o'-war afloat.

In the meantime Tiger Dick seemed to justify my impressions of his character. No better seaman ever set foot upon a holystoned deck. He was firm enough with his men, but I never saw him resort to bullying. He could make even the superstitious smile with the cheery, wondrously catchy tunes that he whistled when the mood was on him;

he seemed never to lose his temper, and he was consistently brisk and cheerful; and within a week Cap'n Fogg was ready to swear by him.

I could quite understand that, for Dick not only performed his work well; he knew how to soothe Cap'n Fogg when that peppery individual's ire rose; and he could do it, too, without appearing to fawn.

Never have I seen a man with more eloquent eyes than Dick's. Something keenly alive and dynamic burned deep in their liquid, dark depths. They would twinkle with appreciation of a joke, shine with gratitude, gleam with quick understanding, mist in sympathy so quickly and so unmistakably that the man could have conversed, it seemed, without a tongue.

**NO MAN EVER** had a more sympathetic listener than Cap'n Fogg enjoyed in his mate when the skipper opened up on his favorite topic—the injustice of the British authorities in their dealings with the colonies.

"Took my own schooner, the *Mary Jane,* not nine months agone," he would say, "on the pretext that she was carrying contraband." And he would snort viciously. "No more than a pair of French gold scales aboard her, too. Seized her, by gum. Not a penny redress. Threatened to put me in jail. Is that justice? Is that fairness?"

"Pirates is what they are, the whole kit an' boiling of 'em!" Dick would reply.

Thus we sailed on, with Cap'n Fogg's hatred of the British burning fiercely, and Dick standing higher and higher in the skipper's estimation each day; while Bruno, the dwarf, carried on as a servant to his master and also did full duty as a member of the crew.

He was a remarkable seaman, too, that dwarf. Handicapped by his twisted legs, his arms were developed to unbelievable proportions. He could mount a line hand over hand as fast as others ran up the shrouds.

Mostly he kept to himself when off duty; he seemed to care for no living man on earth save Dick; and the men soon learned to let him be. One seaman who was bent on teasing him was only saved by Dick when the ugly little man leaped and wrapped an arm like a steel gyve about the astounded sailor's throat. An instant more and he would have choked the pop-eyed joker to death.

"You must remember that Bruno isn't quite right in the head, and has the strength of three," warned Dick, in a confidential aside to a group of the men. "You'd be half cracked, too, like as not, if you'd been catched by Indians off Panama. It was there he lost his tongue and got his legs all shriveled up with fire. 'Twas me who saved him, d'y'see, these many years gone. That's why he dotes on me. He's no more harm than a dog, is Bruno, if you let him be."

I had grown to think so on my own account, by the time we fell into bad weather. A man's repulsive externals grow less revolting after longer acquaintance, and there was something pathetic in Bruno's attitude toward Dick. Ofttimes I have watched his red-rimmed eyes follow the mate about the deck with a look in the depths of them as tender as that in the eyes of a faithful, loving dog.

Then the storms struck us, and the whole complexion of the voyage changed. Worse went to worse. Cholera broke out aboard us; we were blown far to southward of our course; and June found us nearing the edge of the Caribbean.

Death had reduced our crew of twenty-one to seven
men. Only Cap'n Fogg, Tiger Dick, Bruno, Tom Newgate,
Abe Kemp, Jerry Coffin and myself remained alive. We had
rammed a submerged derelict, too, and had sprung a bad
leak forward, so that all were worn and weary with hard
labor at the pumps.

"And have you made up your mind yet which island
you'll put in for, sir?" I overheard Dick inquiring of Cap'n
Fogg one afternoon as the worried skipper bent over his
charts, busy with pencil and dividers.

"I was wishin' one would pop up out of the sea off our
bows!" the captain exploded. "At this rate, we'll be lucky to
reach any. I was thinking, though, of Quanto Bello."

"You've been there?" Dick asked, rather quickly.

The captain said no; it was merely that the charts showed
that island to be the nearest from our present position.

"Right you are, sir," said the mate, looking at the map.
"Only, there ain't a spot on Quanto Bello where you can
careen and calk handy. Coral everywhere. I've been there.
By your leave, sir, I'd say Camano would be best. Good
anchorage there; good water; nice inland harbor, and an
easy sloping beach. It's only a few leagues farther, too."

**"CAMANO?" SAID THE** skipper, frowning. "Don't much
like to enter there. We might fall in with pirates."

"Not now, sir, I shouldn't think."

"Why, I've a chart of the place. It was given to me by
a friend—a court recorder—just after they tried George
Avery for piracy in Boston, these five years back. The pirate
had it in his effects."

"I saw the man swinging in chains, near the old south
buoy," said Tiger Dick, crossing himself. "You've got the

right of it that far, sir. 'Twas on Camano Island George
built his blockhouses. Two years ago I was in that there
bay—Hangman's Bay, they said 'twas called."

"Yes, it's so named in the chart."

"Well, sir, the blockhouses was there then. No signs o'
buccaneers, though. 'Tain't in reason that pirates would put
in there to stay any time, not since George Avery's story
got around."

"That's reasonable, too," agreed the captain.

Thus, through the suggestion of Tiger Dick, we headed
for the landlocked harbor on Camano Island, the former
pirates' stronghold. There, under the lee of the tall hills on
that uninhabited island, we planned to beach, careen and
calk.

We bore away steadily thereafter on the new tack, our
leaking schooner forming the center of a great circle in
which no other mast appeared. For weeks we had not
sighted so much as a tops'l on the horizon, and for a time
we thought that we would reach Camano without having
encountered another craft. But about six bells, on a fine,
clear forenoon, with the bare peak of Tops'l Hill showing
above the white clouds to westward, but several leagues
still between us and our goal, we made out a low-lying,
black hulk, westbound like ourselves, and plowing slowly
through the waters between us and Hangman's Bay!

"A damned pirate, like as not!" Cap'n Fogg groaned
lugubriously.

Tiger Dick had come running on deck, and stood beside
the skipper peering eagerly through his glass. To the naked
eye the strange ship ahead of us was but a blot upon the
water.

"Well, sir, if she *is* a pirate, she's in bad shape," said Dick. "That bit of white you see is nought but a jury rig. She ain't got a stick left in her, she ain't."

"Then I'll stand in closer," Cap'n Fogg decided.

Coming closer, we saw that Dick had spoken truly. The dismasted vessel wallowed along through the glassy, tropical ground swells with but a patch of sail forward. We also saw that she was flying British colors.

"Which doesn't go for much," the skipper grunted. "Easy enough to break out the Union Jack till prey's close in. Then—pop!—out comes the Jolly Roger."

There was, of course, no assurance that buccaneers were not hidden below the decks of the stranger, and we were made doubly suspicious by the fact that the dark vessel was armed and heading straight for Camano. The six nine-pounders on our own ship appeared puny in comparison to the eight heavy black guns our glasses picked out upon the other craft's deck. Some of these we judged to be eighteen-pounders.

"There's this to consider, though," said Tiger Dick, regarding the hulk frowningly: "most ships have guns o' some sort. There's fine, tall trees on Camano, too. Maybe yon craft is just a merchantman who figures to put in and ship new sticks."

Conceding that this was possible, Cap'n Fogg held to his course. Even if there were pirates aboard, they could not maneuver to board us with that jury rig.

"I hope, though," said he, "that she has a good honest crew aboard." He sighed, for our leak was spreading, and we were in the last stages of fatigue. "If that's the case," he concluded, "maybe they'll be glad to trade. Hands for my pumps in return for a tow to Hangman's Bay."

**WE STOOD DIRECTLY,** then, toward the low hull, and steadily overhauled her till our glasses caught the name on her stern. Some one had aptly christened her the *Vulture*.

Relieved as I was by the hope of aid, there was something depressing about that ship which made itself felt despite the distance between us. A decrease in this distance only heightened the sinister impression. Aside from the bit of sail on the jury mast forward, there was hardly a trace of white to alleviate the black of her long, low hull.

"There's something about that craft that I don't like," I remarked.

"So?" said Dick, lowering his own glass. "Well, she ain't no picture, I'll admit. There's suthin' odd about her, though."

"What's that, sir?"

"Why, my son, she ain't flyin' no signal o' distress. I'd call that mighty queer."

"Damned queer," muttered Cap'n Fogg.

As we came still closer in, the strange ship continued to head for Camano Island without showing signs that she was aware of our existence. We could in no wise fathom this, because there was always the risk of the wind changing, and under jury rig the dismasted vessel could hardly hope to wear in unaided.

"Plenty o' people aboard, too, which would have to be fed that much longer if that breeze shifts," said Cap'n Fogg, finally, after another look through his telescope.

Puzzled as we were by this continued aloofness, we were the more intrigued when we thrust our bowsprit within hailing distance. A bulwark divided the after part of the deck from the waist and fo'c's'le. A carved white vulture spread its wooden wings under her sprit; and we saw now that there were British redcoats and prisoners aboard. She was a convict ship!

"Now what in the name o' Davy Jones would a convict ship be doing in these waters, sir?" muttered Dick.

"What I was thinkin'," returned our puzzled, gray-haired skipper. "There ain't but one convict colony, and that's Botany Bay, Australey."

None of us had an answer to the conundrum. Convict ships were almost invariably routed round the Cape of Good Hope when bound for Australia. But in a moment Cap'n Fogg sought a direct answer by raising a megaphone and bellowing, "Where bound?"

We were near enough now to see the figures on the quarter-deck clearly. I noted particularly a slender, foppish chap, leaning nonchalantly against the rail. He was puffing, with an air of boredom, at a long-stemmed, dainty pipe. He outrivaled Beau Brummel in attire, and he eyed our colonial crew with the lazy, contemptuous stare so characteristic of his type. I hated him and his ilk, and had placed him in my black books before I learned his name.

IT WAS NOT this man who answered, but the ship's master, Captain Bradbury. A beefy, red-faced, thickset man, he regarded Cap'n Fogg frostily and deigned to reply:

"We're bound for Camano Island to ship new masts, as any but a Yankee fool could guess. Or maybe you thought as 'ow we were 'eading in to pick flowers—eh, wot?"

The blood thickened in Fogg's lean, sallow cheeks. "I don't give a hoot in Gehenny what you intend to do there!" he ripped out in his shrill nasal tones. "Maybe you hear my pumps a goin'; leastwise your ears are big enough! I've only seven left aboard. Gimme hands for my pumps and I'll tow you in."

"Be damned to you, twice over!" bellowed the red-faced Britisher, swelling mightily. "When I need 'elp, I'll jolly well ask for it, you insolent beggar."

Immediately Cap'n Fogg shoved over the helm, and we veered away, with the two old seadogs exchanging volleys of Billingsgate till both were purple in the face. Meanwhile I could hardly restrain a groan. It was almost time for me to take another turn at the pumps, and I wondered whether I could stick it out.

"Don't you peg out, lad!" whispered Dick behind his upraised palm. "Them hands o' yours are main sore, and no mistake. I'll spell you for an hour."

Small wonder that I had grown fond of the man by this time! All through our troubles he had been like that—a man almost incapable of fatigue, ever ready to spell one of his worn crew, ever ready with a cheerful, heartening word, and as tender as a nurse with the dying men. You may be sure I thanked him heartily with a look as Cap'n Fogg stopped swearing at the Britisher.

"The bigoted old blighter doesn't want us near!" he stormed. "There's something under this won't bear inspection."

"My thought, as ever was," Dick agreed.

Not long afterward, the wind veered, and Cap'n Fogg shook his bony fist at the *Vulture* in high delight. He had not long to laugh, however. That leak was getting out of hand. We now had small hopes of reaching Camano Island on our own account. Cap'n Fogg was, on this account, forced to come down a peg when Bradbury finally signaled for aid.

"Had to come to it, didn't ye?" Fogg taunted, when we once more neared the *Vulture.*

"Wasn't for these lives aboard, you'd never had a chance to rub it in!" Captain Bradbury sulkily retorted.

So it was in a sort of sullen truce that we heaved them a line.

# 4

## A REDCOAT'S GRATITUDE

**WHILE THEY WERE** lowering a boat to send soldiers and convicts aboard, Cap'n Fogg bluntly asked the British sailing master why he was taking the stormy course around the Horn.

"Well," came the gruff reply, "it's none o' your blasted business, but I 'ave cargo for Buenos Aires."

"What do you think o' that?" Fogg asked Dick.

"Why, sir, it's my guess—by the rod—that you could put all his Buenos Aires cargo in your blooming eye."

"Aye, and I'd give a deal to know what's up," added the skipper.

I was myself intrigued and puzzled. There was nothing impossible in Bradbury's insolent explanation, but it was not at all convincing. About the black hull of the gloomy convict ship there hung an air of mystery which was not traceable to the frowning, black muzzles of eight long toms aboard her, ranged in batteries of four on either side; and Bradbury's manner only tended to heighten it.

But there was nothing to be gained by puzzling over the matter; and, indeed, my own thoughts concerning it were diverted soon afterward by the sight of Dick, standing at the rail. He was staring hard at the *Vulture's* longboat, coming up under our counter, and he was laboring under sudden excitement.

"Keelhaul me!" he muttered as I came quietly up behind him. "Can that be Bellew? Long Tom Bellew? So help me Davy Jones, it *is* Long Tom Bellew!"

"Were you talking to me, Mr. Buntline?" I inquired.

He started as though he had not been conscious of my proximity. "Why, no," he returned, giving me a brief, sharp look, followed by a quick and disarming smile. "I was taken aback, Mr. Allen, that's all. By the rod, and you'd be, too. Fancy seein' an old shipmate come to that!"

He shook his great head sadly, and pointed out a man in the boat below us. It was that of a convict, tall and wind-blown, with a scar on one cheek, and a remarkably long nose.

Though he and his comrades wore the white convict garb, with red arrows spangled over the unshapely blouses and trousers, a child of ten could have picked Bellew for a former seafaring man. Life in the crowded, festering hold of the *Vulture* had not served to lessen the tan on his leathery skin, nor to have wiped the marks of the sea from eleven others of the convicts in the boat.

The other eight were landsmen, showing the pallor of London's slums.

"And where did you know him?" I inquired.

Before I could receive an answer. Long Tom looked up from his oar and saw Tiger Dick. The man's jaw dropped. He missed a stroke, and was cursed by the *Vulture's* first mate.

Bellew's green eyes dropped, and he bent to the oar with a will. Yet, at the same time, I saw others among those ex-seamen in convict garb glance up at our rail. On the countenances of several I noted unmistakable signs of amazed recognition.

Instantly the memory of Jed came flooding back to me. While Long Tom Bellew's evil, bleary face was that of a man who would resort to trickery and fawning first to gain an end, he struck me as one who would take to a cutlass as quick as winking. So, too, with the other eleven ex-seamen. With their earrings and their blue tattoo marks, they were a rough lot in appearance, and no mistake.

Tiger Dick must have sensed my thoughts, for at once he said: "Lor' bless me, but this here's a pretty go! Why, there's Joe Darby, and Horse Andrews. Hardy Flintlock, too, as ever was. They sailed under me in the old *Mermaid*—the old *Green Mermaid*, out of Bristol, these three years back. I was first mate, Cap'n Lamb's first mate, and Long Tom, there, was quartermaster. And now I find them here! By the rod, I reckon that's tough. What do you suppose brought them to this?"

"Well, sir, since you've asked me, I wouldn't be surprised if it was piracy," was my answer.

HE REGARDED ME in sidelong fashion, with derision twinkling in his half shut eyes. "Piracy, says you? Why, my lad, there's only one dose the king has for gentlemen o' fortune, and that's a rigadoon at a rope's end on Execution Dock, by thunder! Piracy, my Aunt Mary's foot! Them men are honest enough, as honesty goes these days. And you've been eddicated at Oxford! Don't you know that more than a full half of them poor lads aboard that hell ship has been sent to Botany Bay for nothin' more serious than lifting a pigeon pie?"

I was forced to grant this. Many poor devils were being sent to the "Land Down Under" for seven years' penal servitude for such heinous crimes as striking for a shilling a day more on their pay! And Dick followed his advantage by a withering:

"Why, Mr. Allen, I'm surprised at you! After what King George did to your poor father, you're willing to think the worst of poor devils as wears a convict's clothes? What do that old buzzard care if he stamps a man as a criminal the rest of his days, so he builds up a colony down under? Now you mark my words: I'll ask that there officer so soon as they come over the side, I will. Piracy, my eye!"

The convicts, with a half dozen burly, rum-faced redcoats following them up the companionway, were soon on deck. After them came one Downes, the *Vulture's* first mate, and a tall, ruddy infantry officer who introduced himself as Lieutenant Abercrombie.

"These men are to work your pumps," he said stiffly to Cap'n Fogg, looking them and us over with a cold, distant eye.

Cap'n Fogg's cheeks burned, and I knew that he longed to smite the insufferable young whippersnapper a blow across the mouth. For myself, I raged inwardly with a similar longing. Dissipated, and not overly intelligent in appearance, he nevertheless made it plain by his very manner that we were so much scum in his estimation. But Cap'n Fogg restrained himself, merely saying:

"Mr. Buntline, you'll take 'em below and divide 'em into watches for the pumps."

"Aye, aye, sir," returned Dick. "There's a question, though, I'd like to ask this officer, by your leave." He hooked a thumb at Long Tom Bellew. "That man sailed under me once, sir. Would you mind telling me what brought him to the brig?"

"Why," Abercrombie deigned to answer, coldly, "it was smuggling, if you want to know. He and eleven shipmates were sentenced at Old Bailey together."

"Thankee, sir," said Dick, throwing a triumphant and reproachful look at me. Then, as he started below, Abercrombie turned to Cap'n Fogg and extended a paper.

"A king's warrant to seize and search—if you can't read," he said, insultingly. "Captain Bradbury's orders that I shall search your ship."

"Which maybe will teach you not to loosen your jaw tackle so quick next time," the mate, Downes, leered nastily.

**MY HEART DROPPED** like a plummet as I thought of those guns below. As for Cap'n Fogg I thought he would suffer a stroke of apoplexy.

"Search my ship after signaling for help?" he thundered. "Why, damn your eyes, I—"

"Save your breath, my man!" Lieutenant Abercrombie interrupted. "We'll go below immediately, and you'll let me see your manifest."

Cap'n Fogg suddenly subsided, with a sick air. He told me to produce the manifest, which I did; and when the Britishers had gone below, he remained leaning listlessly against the rail. It struck me to the heart to see him suddenly look so old and gray.

"We'll find some way out of it, sir!" I whispered, hotly.

"We've mighty few hands against such odds, my son," he returned, sadly, staring off to sea.

Raging inwardly as I was, I could not see any way out

of our dilemma just then; and, Abercrombie and Downes having taken some of the convicts to assist them, they soon returned on deck. Abercrombie was smiling faintly and sourly.

"You'll be so good as to turn over your ship to your mate for a time," said he. "You and your supercargo are going aboard the *Vulture* with me."

Cap'n Fogg told me to summon the mate, and I went immediately below. There were but two of the soldiers maintaining an indifferent guard there, one being asleep on some bales; and Dick was talking to Long Tom Bellew at a distance from the pumps when I found him. His eyes were shining strangely.

"I saw them open the boxes," he said, when I spoke, giving his head a gloomy shake. But he accompanied this with a covert wink which mystified me. And no sooner were we out of earshot of the lounging guards than he seized my arm in a tense grip.

"You tell Cap'n Fogg not to grieve," he whispered sharply. "You'll say, 'Dick has a scheme, he has.' That's what you'll say. Seize his ship, will they? Well, we'll see. No, no more. Just tell him Dick has a scheme, and not to worry."

Mystified and thrilled, I followed him on deck, and was soon aboard the *Vulture's* long boat with Cap'n Fogg.

# 5

## TYRANTS OF THE CONVICT SHIP

**ON OUR WAY** to the *Vulture,* dragging heavily astern of the *Bonny Lee,* a garrulous British seaman plied me with questions and in turn gave me information of conditions aboard the convict ship.

The redcoats under Abercrombie numbered but fifteen. Nineteen tars comprised the ship's crew, while of the sixty-odd convicts who started the voyage only thirty-eight had survived an epidemic of typhoid and cholera in the crowded, poorly ventilated hold. Of these, thirty-one were men and the remainder women.

"A rotten, beastly w'y to treat any human beings. I don't care what they've done," the young seaman assured me in guarded tones. "No more convict ships for me, says I. By thunder, but that hold is fit to make you sick. Crowded like sardines, they is."

I was pulling an oar beside the man in the fore seat; Abercrombie, Downes and Cap'n Fogg were in the stern sheets; and I lowered my own voice.

"See here," I ventured to inquire, "what's this ship doing off her course?"

"You ask me another!" he replied, quickly. "It's what a lot of us is asking. We started down the coast of Africa, all regular like, d'y'see. Then what does skipper do but change and point her nose due west."

So that was the case! Cap'n Bradbury's explanation had been a downright lie. Cargoes for Buenos Aires are not routed down the African coast, or picked up in mid-ocean. Something of vital importance had occurred *en route* to make him change his course from the regular route around the Cape of Good Hope to one that must take him the much longer trek around the turbulent Horn.

"What explanation did he give?" I eagerly whispered.

The seaman snorted. "Fancy a hazing skipper like 'im giving any explanation. My eye!"

By this time we were alongside, and had no further chance for conversation till, arriving on deck, I was left standing in the waist, on the port side, while Cap'n Fogg was ushered aft into Bradbury's cabin.

For a moment or two I stood there alone, staring curiously about me, but particularly through the grating in the great oaken door which formed part of the head-high bulkhead amidships. Near this, on the inner side, stood a sentry, but his position did not prevent me from seeing part of the forward deck. Several prisoners were working there under a bo's'n's direction, some painting a gig, others slushing the deck.

Their wan, drawn faces fascinated me, and I was speculating idly upon what had brought this or that one to this pass when the sentry opened the door and a prisoner came through it. Instantly my eyes fastened upon her face, I was conscious of a profound shock.

"That girl going to Botany Bay?" was my amazed thought. "Impossible!"

She wore upon her slender ankle the usual ugly leg iron, and carried, over one shoulder, a chain which ran from the leg iron and ended in a ten-pound ball. Without looking at me, she moved to the rail near by, between two gigs, lowered this ball to the deck, and stared moodily out to sea.

I was astounded, puzzled, shaken to the core of me by the horror and the pity of it. Why, the girl was patrician! Generations of gentle breeding were traced in the delicately etched lines of her aquiline features.

**I LOOKED ABOUT**; the deck was temporarily deserted; and without thought of consequence I spoke impulsively.

"Miss," said I, "what devil's luck brought you here?"

"Stealing," she said laconically then—and turned her eyes once more to seaward.

Color flooded my cheeks. I felt angry, rebuffed. I was ever quick to anger, and about to say something sharp and cutting, when shame overcame me.

"Pray believe me when I say that I did not ask out of casual curiosity," I exclaimed, contritely. "You can't lie to me, either. You never stole a farthing!"

Briefly she smiled at me, and dropped me a tantalizing curtsy. "Ah, but I did, though!" she declared. "It was my own money, I felt—but British law is British law!"

"Do tell me!" I urged.

She looked aft. "You're from that ship ahead, aren't you?" she said. "Well, you must learn that it's against the rules to speak to convicts. I'm waiting here for a most kindly gentleman—a sweet, lovely person, I assure you." Oh, what a wealth of sarcasm and bitterness there was in her tones! "If he appears and sees you, you will be in trouble."

"Is it," I cried, "that tall Beau Brummel?" And I described the foppish chap I had seen upon the poop.

"The same," she answered. "They call him Beau Tyron."

"Devil take him!" quoth I. "I'd risk double and treble trouble for your story."

Her fascinating lashes dropped. "Methinks," she said, demurely, "that you come from Virginia. And have not always sailed before the mast."

"Tell my fortune some more!" I breathed delightedly.

"Then you *did* come from dear Virginia?" she cried, in equal delight. Then her eyes brimmed. "Ah, dear, dear country that I'll not see for seven long years—if ever!"

"You'll see it soon—if I have my way!" I fiercely promised.

Her eloquent eyes thanked me briefly, but in the same breath seemed to say, "What on earth can you do?" After another look aft, she said quickly:

"My name is Gwendolyn Leigh. My father was a Tory, you see, and with all the seditious talk about, and Sons of Liberty forming, and an only daughter who would rather be a good colonial than the queen's lady-in-waiting— why, the poor man was fair distracted. 'Damme, miss!'" she imitated his frightful scowl, " 'I'll make a good Britisher out of you if I die for it, you ungrateful huzzy!' said he. So, when he died, three years ago, there was his will, packing me off to England, bag and baggage."

The will, she explained, contained a stipulation which made an aunt heir to the estate if the girl rebelled and left England voluntarily. It was likewise to revert to the aunt if Gwendolyn married any other than a loyal British subject.

"And you refused to marry that fop Tyron!" I guessed heatedly.

"Yes," she admitted.

**HER LIP CURLED** as she described him as a baronet, an officer of the Guards—in short, a drunken, roistering, dandified duelist, typical of his times.

"It was he," she said, looking out to sea, "who caught me taking what I looked on as part of my own money. From my aunt, you know. So I could return to my own country."

"Whereupon the dog told your aunt?" I cried thickly.

"Not before offering me marriage as an alternative. After that, he told her. So one word led to another, and when I told my aunt I'd rather be a servant girl in the colonies than marry a rum-swilling, bigoted, insufferable British baronet—presto! She sent for the bailiff." The girl's head tossed, and she added, "I told the beefy, redfaced, white-wigged British judge even more—and la! You should have seen his very spectacles fall off!" But her smile was brief. "He sentenced me to seven years in Botany Bay."

"Damnable!" I gritted. "What's Tyron doing here, though?"

"In minor crimes, if a loyal British subject wishes to marry one of us, the woman can be freed on probation. He's obtained leave, and that's why I'm sent out here about every day—at his pleasure."

I was digesting this, and muttering sulphurous curses beneath my breath, when we were startled by a sudden commotion on the forward deck.

Through the grating I saw that one wan, slender prisoner had upset a bucket of paint. The bo's'n was now falling upon the man, cursing viciously. He aimed a murderous kick at the shackled prisoner's stomach, knocking him violently to the deck. Following this, a heavy-footed brute of an infantryman kicked the writhing man again and again as he lay defenseless.

Near by was standing another convict whose resemblance to the poor victim was striking. There was something wistful, something aesthetic, something martyr-like about the finely drawn countenances of those two brothers. The face of the standing convict fairly blazed with horror and indignation; and, weak as he appeared, he leaped to his brother's aid with nothing in his hand but a paintbrush.

The ensuing mêlée fairly set my teeth to grinding. It was not merely that the bo's'n and the soldier knocked the pallid weakling down; it was the sheer delight they evinced while jumping upon both prone figures with their heavy boots! Lieutenant Abercrombie came running on deck, but not to tell the soldier to desist; it was rather to urge the brutes on; and in the end he ordered the victims to be trussed up and lashed with the cat-o'-nine-tails!

"They're the O'Shaughnessy brothers!" whispered the pallid, horrified girl beside me. "Sent out as Irish rebels— poor boys!"

Neither brother was more than barely conscious when trussed up by the wrists to the stump of the mast. They were frightfully lashed across the bare back; at the end raw salt was thrown into the cuts; following which the victims were carried forward and dumped into a tank abaft the companionway.

"What's that for?" I asked Gwendolyn.

"It's filled with salt water," she grimly explained. "It is

supposed to revive them. Sometimes the poor fellows stay down of their own accord. They call it the 'Suicide Tank.'"

**A BLOOD-RED FILM** was gathering before my eyes. I had heard much of British prisons, with their "black holes," their abominable stews, their disciplinary "neck yokes," and their brutal guards. Here I was seeing a sample of it at first hand. Many of the wretches sent to Botany Bay were not guilty of anything worse than a misdemeanor.

When I thought of this girl eating moldy bread, sleeping in that rat-infested hold, lying without covers or pallet in the horrid cell rows in which a British squire would not have stabled a prize hog, my heart seethed with the desire to strangle every redcoat upon the ship.

Then, while my blood was boiling, who should touch me insolently upon the arm but Beau Tyron!

I wheeled about. As through a thick haze I saw that Captain Bradbury and Cap'n Fogg were coming out of the after cabin. But my eyes fastened immediately upon those of the man before me.

Fop, did I say? Ah, but he was. He was the dandy for silver buckles at his knees, was Beau Tyron! He wore a beautiful, pleated ruffled shirt, and a black and glossy wig, quite prettily waved, and tied in a queue at the back of his neck. But I saw now that his attire was responsible for my impression of slenderness; the man was as heavily muscled as myself.

His eyes only met mine for a brief second. It was as though he stared through me, seemed hardly aware of my existence.

"Stand aside, you!" he said—and looked past me at Gwendolyn, oblivious of all save her.

In the man's dark, handsome, brooding face was written the full story of his make-up. He was a seething volcano, a tortured prey to his desires. Even now he gnawed at his pink nails, at sight of her; his nostrils arched; he breathed like a drunken man.

The man was stark, raving mad with love of this girl who flouted him daily, who preferred a foul prison cell in the hold of a hell-ship to sharing his lot.

"Gwendolyn!" he cried.

She looked him up and down with scorn, and turned her back. Whereupon I took a hitch at my sailor's belt, and slapped down his outstretched hand.

"Sirrah," said I, "I like not the shape of your mouth!"

"What?" he muttered. He seemed to realize at last that I was facing him, and the thick blood darkened his neck.

"Out of my way, dog!" he cried, thickly, raising his fist.

*Crack!* My knuckles crashed full upon that sensual mouth; and *crack!* his head struck the deck.

"What's this?" roared Captain Bradbury. Soldiers seized me; sailors picked up Tyron and carried him aft; Bradbury bellowed an order to send Gwendolyn back to the forward deck; and in the next breath the British skipper thundered: "Truss the damned Yankee rebel up! Ten lashes for striking one of his majesty's officers, by thunder!"

They hurried Gwendolyn away, though not before she gave me a tearful look of infinite gratitude and sympathy. A soldier shoved her brutally through the bulkhead door as they lashed me to the stump of the mizzenmast.

**TEN LASHES WAS** what Captain Bradbury of the *Vulture* furiously ordered for me; and ten I received—furiously laid on. I am a strong man, but the scars are upon my back

*Ten lashes with the cat the Britisher ordered*

to this day. How I was enabled to keep from crying out I cannot tell you, for the pain seemed more than mortal man could bear. At the end I was well-nigh fainting, so that I have only a hazy recollection of being helped down the companionway by Cap'n Fogg.

"My poor boy, my poor boy!" were the first clear words I heard from him. He was by no means an iron-fisted skipper at that moment, but more like a kindly father.

"I'll be right as rain very soon," I was able to assure him. "What happened in the cabin, sir?"

"See the sergeant there in the sheets?" said he, with a snort of rage. "To all intents and purposes we're prisoners. If he don't get masts to suit him quick enough, burn him, he's going to take my ship. Confiscate it, by gum, because of those muskets. He hasn't stores enough, he says, to lay to very long, and he's got the law on his side, the robber—what with this embargo against firearms being shipped in. That's the long and short of it, and we're helpless."

"He'll take the ship and maroon us till we can ship masts on the *Vulture?*" I cried. "Is that what he means?"

"That," said Cap'n Fogg, "is exactly what he means."

I kept quiet until we were again in the after cabin of the *Bonny Lee,* and Dick joined us. That worthy cried out in sympathy and sprang to dress my lacerated back. No sooner had the sergeant mounted the ladder and gone on deck than I declared:

"There's something under way that's not legal. Bradbury wants to get away. He'd never desert a ship like the *Vulture,* merely to confiscate a cargo."

"Right you are, my son," said Cap'n Fogg. "It's a rum lay, and you may lay to that."

"But, see here!" cried Dick. "Didn't you tell skipper here as I've a scheme?"

"I hadn't the chance," I said.

Dick's round, fat face was afire with eagerness. Quickly he assured himself that the sergeant was not listening at the door, and he made so bold as to seize Cap'n Fogg's shoulder in his excitement.

"Does you mean to say," he whispered hoarsely, "as you'd let that redfaced lousy swab clean you out, from truck to keelson?"

"You'd see what I'd do if I had hands aboard!" retorted the tired skipper, with sharp asperity.

"Hands, is it?" snorted Dick. "Hands, you say? Well, there's about thirty hands as will sign up with Cap'n Fogg, as quick as winking. Aye, and on half duff at that."

Cap'n Fogg sat up suddenly. "I suppose," said he, "that you mean the convicts!"

"The same," Dick assented eagerly, "as ever was. Though unfortunates is what I'd call most o' them. I told you I knew Long Tom Bellew and them others. You say the word, sir.

Just say the word. Maroon us, will he? Well, I reckon not. I'm an easygoing man, as you've seen; I'm not for hazing and such, not I; but if I don't lay that rum-faced swine athwart, and make him wish he'd never been born, may I be sunk!"

Deep and clever as he was, I think that Dick forgot himself at this juncture; at least his eyes blazed like two tiny points of steel in his great round head.

So I caught my first glimpse of the man's potentialities. It disturbed me. As for Cap'n Fogg, he stared a moment before starting to pace about the cabin in agitation.

"WHAT WOULD YOUR plan be, Mr. Buntline?" he inquired nervously.

"We'll have to go in and calk this leak, that's certain, sir. Well, he'll have to give us hands to shift cargo, and such. Watch as he will, Long Tom can sound out the rest of the boys in irons. We'll surprise 'em at night, we will. What's more, if you say the word, we'll clean out what cargo that swab has and make up for what they captured from your ship last fall."

"No!" snapped Cap'n Fogg. "That would be rank piracy."

"Ah, well, would it, now? Wouldn't it be tit for tat? And here's a point, sir: don't we know war's a comin'? Look at them Boston riots! How do we know the war ain't on already, with companies formin' an' drillin' in every colony?"

"I wish I were certain the boys had struck!" muttered Cap'n Fogg. "I'm not, though."

"But it's self-defense!" argued Dick, the perspiration standing on his brow. "Drat the cargo. Let that slide. But don't let's hang in stays when we've hands only too eager to help us."

"I don't half like releasing some of those hands," Cap'n Fogg demurred. "While many are honest, there's them among 'em would cheerfully cut a man's throat for a shilling, I shouldn't wonder."

"Yes," I granted, "but think of what you saw to-day, Cap'n. We'd be more than repaid for freeing those poor devils that never should have been arrested." I was thinking of nobody but Gwendolyn Leigh.

"We can't be choosers, sir!" Dick declared. "Why, with what few hands we've got, we'd like as not be six months refitting that *Vulture*. Goats and coconuts is what we'd live on, and you may lay to it. Shiver my timbers, but I've a sick heart to think o' that. Aye, and I've a sick heart to think o' my poor men, as once sailed with me, going to Botany Bay. Why, they ain't guilty—begging your pardon—of anything more than you, sir."

Dick appeared to have the right of it. Smuggling is smuggling, whether you break the law with intention to carry contraband French goods into England, or whether you load with muskets for the Sons of Liberty.

"All right," Cap'n Fogg suddenly agreed. His jaw was outthrust. "No piracy, but we'll set every damned convict free and leave the red-faced devil to sweat for it!"

Still thinking of Gwendolyn, I could have hugged him. As for Dick, the man's face shone like a great moon. He nearly broke the captain's hand in a mighty grip.

"You're a skipper after my own heart, by gum!" he cried.

A moment later saw him whistling the strains of the "High Barbaree." He was exuberant. I could not help but remember Jed Morgan's statement. "You never heard a whistle like it, and never will again." That was a true word.

# 6

## BUCCANEERS' ISLAND

**NO SOONER HAD** Cap'n Fogg made his decision than he became once more his terse, decisive, capable self. You would never have guessed that so soft a heart beat within the shell he now donned like a coat of armor. My word, I wish you might have seen the muscles knot in that thin, sharp jaw line, and the spark flash in those steel-gray eyes!

Had it not been for that leak, we might have laid our plans to overpower the soldiers aboard us, and run for it. There was the rub. There were but seven redcoats set to guard us—a Sergeant Holmes and six privates; and our numbers had been swelled by twenty convicts, all presumably eager to escape. What if they were hampered by ball and chain, which they were forced to sling over one shoulder or drag when they moved about? Their arms were free.

But we had rammed a submerged derelict, and the water was gaining, inch by inch, and there Captain Bradbury had us. We must put into Hangman's Bay on Camano or sink.

"Had you broached this subject to this man Bellew before I returned?" Cap'n Fogg asked Dick.

"No more than to ask how many he thought would sign on if I got your permission to strike, sir. There's only a few he'd be doubtful of."

"Well, then, so be it," said the skipper, after a moment of thought. "I'd like to have the choosing of my hands in this, but that isn't possible. Your man Bellew should know by this time who can be trusted to keep his jaw tackle snugged up. Among those convicts, I mean."

"Right you are, sir. You can gamble on Long Tom Bellew."

The skipper nodded, half absently; he was pulling out some old charts. Shortly he produced the one of Camano Island.

I saw that no better place could have been chosen for a pirates' retreat. This was the way of it: the island was about fifteen miles in length and eight or nine miles in width. Except for the bays and inlets, and the curves of the shore-line, the island was almost rectangular in shape.

All round the place the buccaneers had taken soundings, clearly marked upon the yellow bit of parchment, and there were several coves and inlets where ships might have found safe anchorage. There was Execution Inlet, on the west coast; North Cove and Doubloon Bay, on the north shore; and Gig Harbor, on the east.

But a landsman could have picked the pirates' anchorage in a brace of shakes. They had grimly dubbed it Hangman's Bay. You might have sailed round the southern end of the island, and that within a quarter mile of shore, and never have guessed at its existence. That was because a long, narrow island, called Cutlass Sprit, stretched parallel to and within a quarter mile of Camano's southern end, and interposed its four miles or more of heavily wooded ridges between a ship at sea and the entrance to the landlocked bay. At a short distance a stranger would have received the impression of an unbroken shore line.

"When we strike, and how, will depend on what that condemned lobster pot, Bradbury, decides when we wear in," Cap'n Fogg decided. "He'll have to give us hands to shift this cargo, in any case. That 'll give us our chance. In the meantime, just you tip off your man Bellew that mum's the word till we see how the land lies. We can't risk blabbing."

**IT WASN'T LONG** after this before the sun neared the edge of the Caribbean, in the west, and Captain Bradbury sent his mate, Downes, aboard the *Bonny Lee*.

"Just to help the soldiers keep an eye on you," Downes grandly explained. "By the way, Cap'n Fogg, I like the looks of your berth, and, by your leave, I'll take it. You sail your own ship, my orders is; but see that you sail her true, or it 'll be the worse for you."

I was itching all over to be at the man's throat, but the time was not then ripe. What with the inward excitement, caused by the plot I now found myself involved in, and the pain of my lacerated back, the waiting irked me sadly. I burned with eagerness to break the cruel iron band still fastened around that poor girl's slender ankle; and, being feverish with this, and my anticipation of the coming clash, I found myself unable to sleep. So, after some hours of tossing, I rolled out of my berth and went on deck.

By this time we were making headway toward the north end of Camano. Astern of us the moon was peeping from behind a broken bank of dark clouds, and there was something eerie in the silver sheen it spread over our rippling wake. So, too, with the low, black *Vulture,* wallowing in tow behind us, and the dark outlines of the island, off our bow.

In the half-light the heavy growth of trees made of the shoreline a mysterious ebony swath, while above them, and farther inland, rose in silent majesty the stark outlines of four bare and mighty peaks. One the buccaneers had named Old Bailey; another was dubbed Gibbet Spire; a third was called Crow's Nest Peak; while Tops'l Hill was the name they had given the tallest spire of the lot. This was the southernmost hill, rising almost directly behind the northern extremity of Hangman's Bay. I remember well how the moon's light shone upon those bare crags, and how in fancy I could hear the pirates' lookout singing out from the heights of Tops'l Hill that electrifying cry, "Sail ho!"

I was standing at the rail, busy with my thoughts, when Dick, who had been on watch, and was just now being relieved by old Tom Newgate, came and placed a warm brown hand over my own.

"Ah, but that was a fine, brave thing you did for that girl, my lad!" he declared. "Cap'n Fogg has been a tellin' me about it. We'll even up for that poor back, and you may lay to it, my boy."

"Have you spoken to Bellew?" I asked him.

"I have, and no mistake. Just you rest easy. If you can't sleep, just you slip into' the cabin, and let me dress that back again."

I promised him that I would, and he went below at once, leaving me still on deck.

Well, I had been there but a few minutes longer when old Tom Newgate came over and stood beside me at the rail. The helmsman, Jerry Coffin, was out of earshot.

"How are ye feelin' now, my lad?" old Tom wanted to know.

"Better," I said. "And has the captain told you yet?"

Tom cleared his throat, and spat.

"He has," he returned in strangely troubled tones.

I looked at him quickly.

**OLD TOM WAS** generally an uncommunicative fellow. For a man of his age he was remarkably spry, and had proved to be a most efficient bo's'n; but whenever he was off duty he seemed to prefer his own company to that of others.

I have seldom seen a man more capable with tools; he seemed to love the very feel of wood; and at odd hours he was forever whittling at such gim-cracks as chains, whittled out of a solid block of oak, or tumbling acrobats that performed under the impetus of a revolving windmill. A square-set, leather-colored, thoughtful old seaman, was Tom, with a quid forever bulging one clean-shaven cheek, and a broad, wrinkled visage that would have passed for a symbol of honesty anywhere.

"Why, Tom," said I, "what's worrying you? You're not afraid of our success, are you?"

He wouldn't meet my eye. He coughed, and scraped his feet, and stared aloft, and then out to sea, and finally spat again.

"It ain't that," he said presently. "Maybe it's because I'm getting old. Maybe it's because them pumps has wore me down. Maybe it's jest them mountings there, so solemn-like and—and mystified, kind of. I don't rightly know. There's something—well, anyway, I feel blue about this here deal, I do."

"Tom," I charged, "you're trying to tell me something!"

He started, I thought guiltily. He only gave me one swift glance, and then, after a look at the cabin, shook his head.

"No!" he said gruffly, after the manner of a man who has suddenly made up his mind. "It's just that I don't feel well, I don't."

"Tom," I repeated, "you know something. Now, you're an honest man, or I'm a dunce. Come now: back in Jed Morgan's public house you and Dick greeted one another as old shipmates. Well, then, were you shipmates when he sailed with this Bellew?"

"Why, yes, son, to be sure," he answered readily enough. "On the—yes, on the old *Green Mermaid,* to be sure. What o' that?"

"They're a hard-looking lot, Tom, that's all."

"Maybe," he grunted. Still staring off to sea, he said at last: "Forty-five years at sea, I've been, and I'm getting old. Ah, but the things I've seen! Mates a dyin' with scurvy, and cutlasses swingin', and brisk messmates as got crazy after the jolly sov'rings, and ended up at Execution Dock, by thunder! You'd have your hair on end if I was to tell you all I've been through, I shouldn't wonder.

"Well, son, that's what's the matter. All I want now is to end my days in peace ashore. A little carpenter shop— that's what I wants. And now—well, here's a shindy in the wind, and who knows but what I'll never get that carpenter shop, but go where I've seen so many go before—some to feed the fishes, and some to the gibbet, but all to the long shore?"

"So that's all?" I cried, my suspicions lulled. I clapped him on the back. "You'll live to get that shop," I assured him. "I feel it in my bones."

**I LEFT HIM** there, making my way to the little room in the after cabin where Dick held forth. It so happened that I came upon him with his upper garments removed; and I exclaimed in amazement as I noted a horrible scar in his corded, muscular back. "How on earth did you ever survive that?" I cried.

"That?" he said easily. He smiled and turned toward me. "Look here," he directed.

I gasped, for his torso was literally intermeshed with ghastly scars. "What is a little cut like that one aft?" he said, showing his even white teeth. "No, I didn't get them fighting, son. Leastwise, not with seamen. 'Twas the Indians did that to me, time I saved Bruno, the dwarf. But you never mind them scars. You'll have some o' your own to carry, I shouldn't wonder."

With that he donned a shirt, and insisted on redressing my burning back with a cooling lotion. This and a drink he mixed for me soon eased my pain and allowed me to drop into a sleep.

When I awoke the sun was shining warm and fair upon a smiling sea, and we were near the southern end of the island. In daylight the air of mystery was dissipated, and the prospect of landing ashore was most alluring. Along the eastern coast there stretched a golden beach, upon which the racing blue combers broke into cascades of sparkling white. Mangos and palm trees furnished a brilliant green contrast to the gleaming, yellow sands, abetted by patches of broad ferns; live oaks, pine and mahogany trees thrived thickly upon the plateaus and promontories; and here and there were green meadows and restful glades, most inviting to a man who has been long at sea.

I remember how my nostrils arched as the gentle offshore breeze bore us the odors of flowers, and how I longed to quench my thirst in the cold, blue waters racing down into Hangman's Bay from the heights of Tops'l Hill.

But the pleasant aspects of the land were temporarily put out of mind a moment later when my eye fell on a coral reef off the eastern end of Cutlass Sprit. Upon it a square-rigged ship had long since impaled herself. She had broken in two amidships, but so firmly spiked was she that the surf had not been able to dislodge her.

Kelp and seaweed filled the split in her hull; one mast still stood, while another banged to and fro in the surf alongside; at least three of her guns were still lashed in place on the deck.

"What do you make of that, Mr. Buntline?" I asked as Dick came up, with his faithful Bruno behind.

"That?" Dick said—and it seemed to me afterward that his voice was a bit off key. "Why, that would be a pirate's hull, and I shouldn't wonder. See there? They've painted out the name on her stern. Afore they abandoned her, I'll gamble. Yes, sir, I'd say they was making for here when a storm disabled them. She ain't been here more'n a few months at most, is my guess."

The tongueless dwarf was making rapid signs with his fingers, and Dick answered him in kind before turning back to me.

"If ships could talk!" he said, with something of a sigh. Then he added: "Ah, there's Cap'n Bradbury puttin' off the *Vulture* in a gig. We'll know soon what's what, my lad."

# 7

## THE LAST STRAW

CAPTAIN BRADBURY, AS soon as he came aboard, rasped: "I haven't a chart of this here island. I don't like the looks of that wreck there, either."

When Cap'n Fogg gruffly asked him why, Bradbury hotly exclaimed: "Why? Suppose there was a gang of pirates gone ashore off that wreck? That's why."

Thereupon Cap'n Fogg showed the man his chart, and it was decided that both ships would drop anchor off Cutlass Sprit and tow in with the tide. In the meantime Bradbury was to take a boatload ashore and reconnoiter.

"No use in sticking our heads into a trap," said he.

"Maybe he's right," said Dick. "At the same time, something tells me those fellows got off. The boats are gone off that wreck, you'll notice. There would not be much sense in buccaneers waitin' here for ships to put in, either. There wouldn't be one in a blue moon."

In a few hours Bradbury returned, reporting that he had examined a fort overlooking the lower part of the harbor, and found it deserted and without signs of occupation for several months past. So, as the tide started to make, we manned the boats and started in.

Once between Cutlass Sprit and the mainland it was

more than ever apparent that the buccaneers had had the best of it when molested. Upon the south shore of the mainland, at the top of a steep hill, they had built a heavy log fort, from the portholes of which a half dozen black muzzles still protruded.

These effectually commanded the whole lower, or southern, half of Hangman's Bay. You could sail into this lower bay around either end of Cutlass Sprit; by passing between the Sprit and the southwestern corner of the island, called Bowsprit Bluff, if you rounded the western end, or by passing between it and Kidd's Neck, if you selected the longer and narrower entrance to eastward; but in either case those guns raked you fore and aft.

After entering the lower harbor, there was still another passage to navigate before the upper part of the bay was reached. This passage was about one-eighth of a mile wide, nearly a mile long, and lay between Kidd's Neck and the mainland. It twisted tortuously from the lower bay toward the northeast.

The eastern side of the upper harbor was formed by the long, narrow neck, or spit, which lay between the bay and the east end of Cutlass Sprit; and it was so narrow and twisted that it really did suggest the probable appearance of Kidd's neck after his drop from the gallows at Execution Dock.

Once you worked through the passage, you found yourself in a safe retreat, about a mile wide and three miles or so in length. Tall trees on the ridges of Kidd's Neck completely screened you from the view of those at sea, while from Tops'l Hill, rising not far from the northern end, you could scan the horizon at all points of the compass.

We picked up a bit of breeze to help us going in, and by noon observation were well within the sheltered cove. There we saw how the buccaneers had further prepared themselves for defense, as well as a long stay ashore in case of need.

Emptying into the harbor, from the northwest, was a shallow creek. Just beyond this the north shore started its curve across the upper end of the inlet. Two hundred yards or more to eastward of the creek mouth was a cleared slope, and on this, some distance inland, they had thrown up a palisade and blockhouse. Aside from the weeds that had grown round the stumps, the log house appeared to be in fairly good shape.

**IT WAS NEAR** the mouth of this creek in the upper harbor that Captain Bradbury decided to beach the *Vulture*, while we found a suitable spot some distance to southward, on the same—or western—side of the harbor. Off these respective points the two ships came to anchor, to wait for the tide; and immediately Captain Bradbury was rowed to the *Bonny Lee*, bringing Lieutenant Abercrombie with him.

"Bring that prisoner Bellew and the man Andrews here," he told a soldier when he came on deck.

"Now what?" muttered Cap'n Fogg under his breath.

"I've found that these two men are handier, as riggers, than any of my own seamen," Bradbury told Fogg, when the two convicts appeared. "I'll take 'em ashore with me to look those trees over."

When the *Vulture's* gig was finally beached, the sailors at the oars remained aboard. Captain Bradbury, Lieutenant Abercrombie, the mate Downes and the two convicts.

Bellew and Andrews, went ashore. They disappeared at once into the thick trees.

"Something odd in that!" muttered Cap'n Fogg.

"Well, maybe not, sir," said Dick. "Long Tom and Horse Andrews certainly are good riggers."

"Doubtless. What interest has Abercrombie got in rigging, though?"

Dick's answer was a shrug; and Bradbury's exploring party was ashore over two hours, before it returned.

"Well, we found suitable pines," Bradbury declared, quite jovially. "So I'll refit the *Vulture*."

But our own plight was not materially bettered. Save for Bellew and Andrews, the prisoners aboard us were to remain at our disposal, under the same guard, until we were fit for sea. In the meantime the remaining prisoners and the *Vulture's* crew of nineteen would be put to felling trees and working them down the slope with peavies, while camps would be pitched ashore.

"After you've loaded, though," Captain Bradbury said bluntly, "you'll stay here till the *Vulture* is fit for sea."

"And then?" said Cap'n Fogg.

"It shouldn't be more than three weeks afore the *Vulture* is ready. Then I'll put some o' my hands aboard you, and some o' these prisoners, with a guard. From here we'll sail smack in to Kingston, and I'll turn you and your precious cargo over to the governor of Jamaica."

"Ha!" snorted Cap'n Fogg, as soon as the Britisher had gone. "That clears the decks. We'll strike as soon as we've refloated."

# 8

## REBELLION

**THAT AFTERNOON BOTH** ships were beached, and propped on even keels. Camps on the yellow sands were pitched under the shade of palms and white tarpaulins. I noted that the women, in the *Vulture's* camp, had been given the task of cooking, and were somewhat isolated from the men, and I was all for slipping down there, under cover of darkness.

"Miss Leigh can tell me a lot about which of these convicts are to be trusted not to inform," I argued to Cap'n Fogg.

"And if you get caught, they'll put you in irons," he returned. "We need all we can trust when we strike."

Forced to recognize the common sense in his stand, I gained some contentment in the thought that Gwendolyn was at least enjoying the contrast with those horrible quarters aboard the *Vulture;* and so I plunged into the work at hand, afire with eagerness to hasten the day of her release.

From the time we landed, the work progressed steadily. By day the harbor was alive with the *chock* of axes, or the sound of hammers within our hull, or the "Yo-ho-ho!" of lusty tars hauling away at block and falls. At night the camp fires cast their cheery glow out across the tranquil waters, and song fests were in order at both camps. No more lovely spot could have been found to come ashore in.

Even the convicts were elated. Their gloom perceptibly lessened; their cheeks showed more color; they looked improved in every way.

Moreover, we were living like kings, on mangos and wild bananas, sweet yams and turtles' eggs and fresh fish; we likewise bagged some fresh wild hog meat, and venison, and enjoyed a liberal ration of grog; and under such conditions, we made headway so rapidly that we saw our way clear on the fifth day to refloat that night, if all went well.

**THE HIGHEST TIDE** did not come to flood that evening until after dark. Captain Bradbury, being anxious to place all hands at work on the *Vulture,* had been agreeable to our reloading by lighters as soon as we had launched. It was then we were to strike; and as the hour approached, I labored under an excitement so tense that I feared my very nervousness would give the Britishers warning.

But Dick seemed not in the least worried. He had confided, he said, in none of the convicts save his old shipmates; and, nothing occurring to delay us, six bells—eleven o'clock—found the *Bonny Lee* again riding at anchor, some two hundred yards off shore.

The lighters were alongside, the bales and boxes which we had removed from the forehold were once more on deck and in the process of being lowered through the hatch. Ten convicts were below, acting as stevedores, under Cap'n Fogg. Eight were on deck, slinging boxes. Dick was in charge there, and with him were Tom Newgate, Abe Kemp, Coffin and the dwarf Bruno. I stood near by, lantern and manifest in hand.

Sergeant Holmes had brought all six of his squad aboard. Two of these soldiers were on watch—one on deck, and one below, with Cap'n Fogg. Sergeant Holmes lolled beside the starboard rail, smoking a pipe; the other four soldiers had been allowed to stretch out on some tarpaulins under the foremast boom.

All round the island it was very quiet. Only a few coals remained of the camp fires ashore. Apparently all of Bradbury's camp were sunk in slumber save a lone sentry who paced slowly back and forth past the tarpaulins under which the convicts slept. In the east the moon was rising, its round edge just peeking up over the tree tops which stood so dark and still on the plateau at the base of Tops'l Hill.

It had been agreed that Dick was to give the signal; and at last I saw him covertly nudge Bruno. The dwarf was behind his master, and the sleepy sentry facing the mate. Behind Dick's back I saw his fingers conveying a message to the dwarf.

Bruno immediately picked up a rope and started coiling it. Meanwhile he moved nearer Sergeant Holmes. Then said Dick:

"Ah! We'll soon be ashore now, my lads. Here's but another slingload to go below."

"A good thing it is, too," growled Holmes.

At that moment Dick leaped full upon the sentry. The stupid ruffian's heavy flintlock was whipped from his lax hands so swiftly that he could but gape and stare.

Simultaneously the dwarf was upon Holmes like a catamount, throwing the heavy coil of rope about the man's arms and shoulders. A hairy paw nipped Holmes's startled cry in the bud, and brought him crashing to the deck.

In the same breath Dick was saying, in low clear tones:

"If you so much as stir, my lad, you're sunk. Coffin, truss up this swab, Tom, get the others' muskets, and lively."

I had leaped to aid Tom Newgate in snatching the muskets of the sentries who now stirred on the tarpaulins: there was a scuffle below; and in a brace of shakes we had the situation in hand. It had been surprisingly easy—so far.

# 9

## TO THE ATTACK

**"ALL'S WELL BELOW!"** Cap'n Fogg called up to us.

"All's shipshape here—or soon will be," Dick returned. "Lively now, lads. Remember, you redcoats—let me hear one of you sing out, and you'll hear the echo in hell. Gag 'em, lads, and truss 'em well." Then he wheeled on Bruno, who still crouched above Holmes's slack form. "Let go there, Bruno, and truss the man."

Bruno reluctantly released his grip on Holmes's throat, and arose, as Cap'n Fogg popped on deck.

Some of the convicts had not been taken into the plot, but those on deck were not slow to grasp the situation. One of the London criminals snarled and pushed Coffin aside, smashing at the bound sentry's head with a belaying pin. The soldier, he whose heavy boots had crushed the Irishman, O'Shaughnessy's ribs, flopped to the deck with a broken skull.

His fall was followed in a flash by that of the convict. Cap'n Fogg had seized a musket from the sentry below, and with it he had felled the prisoner.

"That's what I'll deal out to him who murders except in fair fight!" he gritted, glaring about him like a wolf at bay. "Now mark my words, the lot of you: I'll set you free, as I've

agreed, but you'll remain as hands before the mast till I've
clapped you somewhere safe ashore in the colonies. There'll
be no settling of old scores, unless we find a fight on our
hands ashore. Below now, and lively to knock off irons."

"Aye, aye, sir," returned some of the former seamen,
promptly.

We found a key in the sergeant's pocket, and soon
released the eager, excited prisoners from their irons.

**"NOW, MEN," SAID** Cap'n Fogg, when one of the boxes of
muskets had been broken open, and cutlasses and pistols
brought, ready to be served round, "I've a thing or two to
say. Makes no odds how we do it—every man we have to
kill here will be charged against us by the British authorities as another murder. Amen, so be it. But I'm acting
strictly because I'm in a clove hitch, and doing what I think
is right. Not a dollar's worth of dunnage do I plan to take
off that *Vulture*. That's flat. Not a man do I plan to kill
except that fighting may make it necessary. Is that all clear?"

"Aye, aye, sir," growled Hardy Flintlock. "It's fair enow.
Only, we've had main hard treatment for a bit o' smuggling—asking your pardon."

"I'll grant that. And I'll say this: if we're successful in
taking the other camp, you can bring any of those soldiers
before me for trial as you have just charges against. But fair
trial they'll get, and don't mistake me."

"That's fair enow," repeated Hardy.

"Then," said the skipper, "point out to me any informer
here that you fear may give warning before we get there."

Without hesitation several of Hardy's old messmates
pointed to one man. He whined and protested, but was
gagged and bound, and left aboard with the soldiers, for

safe keeping. Abe Kemp and Jerry Coffin were left to guard them.

With this done we took to the boats. Five of us were from the *Bonny Lee's* old crew: and our numbers had been swelled by seventeen convicts, so that we now boasted of twenty-two.

Nevertheless we took no chances, and once ashore, moved toward the sleeping camp with extreme care, keeping well within the trees. When finally opposite the convicts' tarpaulin, Hardy Flintlock and a companion crawled forward.

The sentry was at the north end of the camp. Hardy and his mate safely reached the shelter of some bushes near the southern end of his beat. When the soldier wheeled and started trudging slowly toward the two, they crouched low and waited, motionless.

At last the slowly moving soldier reached the end of his beat. When he wheeled in his stiff military fashion to retrace his steps northward, Hardy and his mate leaped.

The man's musket was discharged with a thunderous report. It set the echoes to crashing back and forth across the quiet bay.

But the shot went harmlessly into the air. Under Hardy's musket stock the sentry came down with a crash like that of a felled bullock.

He had not struck the ground when Dick roared out from the depths of his mighty chest, "Over the side, all-l-l-l hands!"

It was a signal for a charge that swept toward the camp like maddened bulls.

# 10

## WITH GUN AND CUTLASS

**STRETCHING FROM NORTH** to south along the shore of the harbor the sleeping Britishers lay as follows: Captain Bradbury under tarpaulins with Downes and two other mates, also Lieutenant Abercrombie and Beau Tyron, at the northern end; next, the *Vulture's* crew of nineteen tars; then the other eight infantrymen of Abercrombie's command; adjoining them those convicts not allotted to the task of repairing our *Bonny Lee;* and the women at the extreme southern end of the camp.

We were stretched out in a line parallel to the camp, and facing eastward. Tiger Dick had been given command of a group on our left, facing Bradbury's headquarters; Cap'n Fogg had the center, which was to fall on the British sailors; and old Tom Newgate led the right flank, heading for the sleeping soldiers.

The discharge of the sentry's musket had roused all hands, and before we crossed the space between the trees and the camp, a number of the British sailors and soldiers had started up, weapons in hand.

In the bright moonlight I saw at least two of the sailors and three of the soldiers raising their pistols or muskets to fire—when suddenly I stumbled over a rope and pitched headlong.

That action was swift. Before I could arise several shots reechoed across the lagoon. Savage yells, choked curses, and the screams of frightened women rent the air.

I was in Cap'n Fogg's squad, and leaped to my feet in time to see a comrade fall upon a British sailor who faced him with upraised cutlass. Before the cutlass fell a shot struck the sailor full in the breast. He dropped his weapon, clutched at his breast, and slowly toppled upon another British tar who was struggling to free himself from a tangle of blankets.

At the same time Cap'n Fogg was crying: "Throw down your arms, you fools—the game's up!"

Before I had taken three strides this seemed to be apparent to the majority of the British tars, still fuddled and dazed with sleep. Most of them threw down their arms, or, caught in blankets, made no attempt to defend themselves, raising their hands instead and calling for quarter.

The soldiers were caught in like predicament. Those who resisted were rushed by groups of convicts, who fell upon them with the fury of tigers.

The cries for quarter from the remaining soldiers rose even higher than the fearful screams of pain; but over and above all I could hear the voices of Dick and Captain Bradbury, at the north end of the camp.

"Throw down your arms!" roared Tiger Dick.

"To hell with you!" thundered the British skipper, his pistol vomiting flame and smoke.

There were no cries for quarter there. Bruno, Hardy Flintlock and a half dozen of our released convicts found the *Vulture's* three mates and Abercrombie, the lieutenant, upon their feet, ready with cutlasses and blazing pistols.

Two of the convicts fell, and one of the mates went down; then Dick's cutlass met that of Captain Bradbury's with a slithering crash, and the men behind him rushed upon their old enemies with oaths to chill the blood.

The terrific cut aimed by Tiger Dick at the British skipper snapped off the Englishman's blade as though it had been a match stick. Bradbury bellowed in fury and tried to close, but Hardy Flintlock brought the oxlike figure to its knees with a smashing, downward blow that bit through the shoulder to the breastbone.

As another of the other Britishers fell upon Dick, Hardy Flintlock and Bruno, the dwarf, hacked ferociously at the wounded Bradbury. Such utter viciousness I had never before witnessed. They lopped off one of his arms, split his head, and slashed him in a dozen other places.

Dead he must have been before he toppled like a heavy oak, yet they were leaping upon him and continuing to hack at his bloody remains when I reached Cap'n Fogg.

**ALL RESISTANCE IN** our immediate vicinity had by this time ceased, and Cap'n Fogg started on the run toward the combatants to northward, calling on three of us to follow. We had barely started when the last of Bradbury's officers fell. Bradbury was, of course, stone dead; so were all three mates; and Lieutenant Abercrombie was unconscious and bleeding from a dozen wounds when we came up.

Dick had subsided on a camp stool, panting heavily and wiping the perspiration from his face. Tyron was struggling in the arms of two of the convicts. They were berating him for a fool, and cautioning him to cease resisting, when Bruno snarled horribly and leaped at him, cutlass raised.

"Avast there!" cried Cap'n Fogg, tripping the dwarf. He aimed a pistol at the same time.

"This man," Fogg continued, indicating Tyron, "is disarmed. Let me see him who'll lay a hand on him!"

Bruno growled menacingly, but subsided; but a commotion near by caused the skipper to wheel. There was Hardy Flintlock moving toward an English sailor who stood with his arms aloft. Hardy was a fearful figure. He was spattered with blood; he seemed fairly drunk with it; he breathed stertorously and staggered heavily in his ungainly stride.

"Quarter!" pleaded the frightened tar.

"Quarter!" Hardy thickly mocked him. "Ah," he went on, in a sort of singsong, " 'but the quarter that we gave them was to sink them in the sea!' "

With that he struck a murderous blow at the head of the defenseless man.

This was the signal for a stampede among the *Vulture's* crew. The intended victim dodged and ran for his life. Hardy started after him; others among the released convicts selected victims against whom they had grudges, and gave pursuit; and in a twinkling of an eye the most depraved of the rascals under Fogg's command would have been completely out of hand.

The skipper stood not on ceremony. He raised the pistol and let fly with one barrel, aiming straight at Hardy. The bullet burned the blackguard's tattooed forearm. Away went his cutlass, knocked from his numbed fingers. He stopped dead in his tracks. Slowly he turned toward Fogg, a silly, shocked, incredulous expression on his heavy blue face.

It brought the rest of the mutineers up standing, as well. For a second there was dead silence.

"I didn't mean that shot for your hand, either!" declared the skipper, his voice cutting through the air like a knife. "Next man cuts down an unarmed prisoner will swing at the yardarm before his cutlass is dry!"

Black looks and muttered curses greeted him on all sides, save from a bare handful of our new crew; but Cap'n Fogg quickly improved the situation by summoning to him Tom Newgate and four of our convicts who appeared to be honest, sober and wholesome fellows. Then he called out: "This way, all you men off the *Vulture!*"

The white-faced Englishmen were quick to obey, and Cap'n Fogg struck another blow while the iron was hot.

"Every man Jack of my crew this way to stack arms!" he commanded.

**THOUGH FROWNING AND** looking sidewise at one another, our crew started coming up, one after another. With them they brought their own and the captured weapons. The four honest fellows and Tom Newgate were told their arms were to be retained, and that they were to stand guard over the muskets and cutlasses till further orders.

All this time the women and those among the male convicts who were still in irons had remained in their tents. I was anxious to speak to Gwendolyn, but, the skipper directing me to aid with the wounded, I could not go at once.

In addition to Bradbury and his officers, two of the soldiers would never speak again. There were also six wounded—Abercrombie, a sailor, one soldier, and three of our convicts. With these last I fell to work.

Dick had moved over beside the captain by this time, and at a request from the mate the two stepped away, but not so far that I could not catch their low words.

"If I might suggest it, sir, I would not be too brisk with these lads just now." Dick nodded at our men, who, at the captain's orders, were sullenly gathering wood to stoke up the fires. "They've been hazed a long time, sir. Now, a bit of fling till morning won't do them—and us—no harm."

"I suppose not."

"If I might make another suggestion, sir," Dick resumed, "I'd tie up those swabs from the *Vulture's* crew, along with them sojers, and clap 'em under hatches aboard the *Bonny Lee*."

The skipper approved of this as a good suggestion. He didn't want to leave the *Vulture's* crew ashore while the *Bonny Lee* was getting under weigh; there was the fort overlooking the lower harbor to think of.

"Once outside, I'll send 'em back ashore," he said. "I'd sail to-night, by gum, if there was a capful o' wind. There isn't, so I'll let the men have their little fling. You may tell off some of the hands, Mr. Buntline, to take our prisoners aboard the *Bonny Lee*. Truss them and leave Kemp, Coffin, and"—here his eye roved over our new crew—"that man there to guard 'em." He indicated a convict who appeared to have been a landsman.

"Aye, aye, sir," responded Dick.

In a jiffy Dick had told off a half dozen of our men, handed them muskets, and marched away to the boats with the captives. They included Tyron, sixteen sailors, and the remaining soldiers.

The sailor and soldier being only slightly wounded, I had sent them along with Dick, and was attending to a more serious cut in the arm, suffered by one of the convicts, when four men brought Abercrombie in a blanket. I saw that there was no hope for him. But he had regained consciousness and was struggling to speak.

"I'm listening," Cap'n Fogg assured him, bending over the dying man.

"Treasure!" gasped the wounded lieutenant. "There's treachery here. Treasure—"

Here his eyes filmed, his throat filled, and he died.

# 11

## DANGEROUS UNDERCURRENTS

"**NOW, WHAT THE** devil do you make of that?" muttered Cap'n Fogg, straightening up. He removed his wig and scratched his bald head.

"There was something afoot, sir, I'll be bound," volunteered one of the more honest-looking convicts. "The whole ship was puzzled about it."

"You mean because Bradbury changed course, my man?"

"That's it, sir. I wouldn't wonder but what there *was* treasure here, sir, this being a pirate's hang-out."

"Does any one here know anything about it?" Fogg demanded.

All the surrounding faces appeared blank or wore an air of reserve. Near by, on the sloping shore, Dick and his captives had been about to embark in the *Vulture's* boats; but they were within earshot of our fire, and now Dick returned briskly toward us, his eager eyes fastened upon the skipper's face.

"Did I hear something about treasure, sir?" he asked politely.

Cap'n Fogg repeated Abercrombie's dying words.

"So!" Dick said slowly, after digesting this. He smiled skeptically. "Well, Cap'n Bradbury's dead now, and gone below: he knows by now he came on a wild-goose chase, and you may lay to it."

"What makes you think so?"

"Why, sir, maybe some one's sung Cap'n Bradbury a song of treasure here. A chucklehead as had never run across a gentleman o' fortune might easily believe they stowed their blunt on places like this. Only, them as I have seen ashore, in places like Porto Bello, why, they wasn't the lads to save, not them. A coach and six, and a hogshead o' rum beside the driver, and to sea again in rags. That was their style; easy come and easy go: and if ever any of them swabs ever buried blunt, it was because they was close pressed."

"My opinion, too," Cap'n Fogg instantly replied. He addressed the men. "We sail on the morning tide, men, if there's a bit of wind. After you've buried the dead, you can broach a cask of rum." Here he was interrupted by a cheer. "Mr. Newgate," indicating old Tom, "will be recognized from now on as second mate. You'll tell off men to bury the dead and release those poor lads who are still in chains, Mr. Newgate. And, Mr. Buntline, you'll bring back dungarees from the slop chest for these men who'll want to chuck these convict togs."

"Aye, aye, sir," said Dick; while old Tom, apparently unable to believe his ears, rubbed his chin and stared almost stupidly.

"You meant as I'm to be second officer, sir?" he gasped.

"Exactly, Mr. Newgate."

"Well, I—" old Tom stammered. "Well, I— Well, thankee kindly, sir."

"And now," Cap'n Fogg said briskly, nodding for me

to follow, and addressing Dick, "I've a word to say to that man Tyron."

We three started down the beach toward the boats. "You took the right lay, Mr. Buntline," the skipper said quickly, in low tones. "While there may be something in that treasure yarn, we'd have a mutiny, like as not, if the men believed it."

"Just what I spoke up for, sir," Dick quickly responded. **THERE WAS NO** chance for further words, since we drew near the waiting captives. Among them, though a little to one side, stood Beau Tyron, caressing his chin moodily. He gave us an ugly frown.

"You are an officer on leave, I understand," said Cap'n Fogg.

"An army captain—yes. What of it?"

"This of it: give me your parole, and I'll give you the use of a cabin aboard the *Bonny Lee* till I set you back ashore."

"Perhaps you think you can bribe me to be a witness when you're in court for piracy and murder," Tyron soon returned. "You'll get no parole from me. If I see a chance to lay you by the heels, that's what I'll do, my man."

"So be it," returned Fogg, not without a trace of admiration. He directed Dick to proceed, and took me off a short distance down the beach. Giving me one of the sergeant's keys, with which to release the women, he added:

"You see how things are, my lad. I've had to take hide with tallow, and which is good honest tallow in that mess of broad-arrow swabs, I've had to take snap judgment on. You talk to that girl. There's a knowing, observant girl, or I'm mistaken." He removed his hat and wig, and rubbed his head. "I don't mind confessing it, son—I'm worried."

"Captain," I said, "I've something to tell you." And I told him Jed Morgan's story.

He listened intently to the end. "I don't like that," he said. "I'll give Dick the benefit of the doubt, though. The man had the best of recommendations from the port captain of Liverpool. We will keep a bright lookout, however. Quick, now, and learn what you can."

Off I went, as briskly as you please, and my heart thumping. Some one had already released the remaining prisoners, and three of the women were dancing with men upon the sand, while others laughed and shouted incoherently, the men whirling their irons round their heads and throwing them out into the water. Still others were weeping tears of joy and seizing this hand and that to shake in their ecstasy. Even the men at work on the graves were shouting in glee.

I found Gwendolyn sitting quietly under a tarpaulin. "I've been waiting for you to come," she said simply, holding out a slender hand. She shook mine, much as a boy might have done, letting her eyes, rather than effusive words, express her gratitude and joy at her release.

There were any number of things I wanted to say, but time was pressing, and perforce I stated my mission, and told her of the attack and our plans. She at once accompanied me to a point near by, from which we could see most of the figures near the roaring fires, upon which some were tossing wood.

"Why Captain Bradbury came here is a mystery to me," she said. "But this I know: among the convicts I would trust—well, not more than ten of the men."

These she named and pointed out, after which we went

to the captain's fire, not far from the bows of the *Vulture*.
All the new crew, save the guard set over the weapons,
had foregathered round two fires that were blazing some
distance to northward.

**SHORTLY THE SKIPPER** and Tom Newgate returned
from reading a prayer over the dead, and I gave them her
opinions.

"That's good," said Cap'n Fogg. "I will see that those
hands are told off to relieve the guard."

Casting an eye over our carousing, excited crew, he
nodded at me reassuringly. They were roaring a chorus
which ran:

> "Now, when my t'other leg was lopped.
>
> Well, for a bit o' fun,
>
> With it in hand, why up I hopped.
>
> And rammed it in a gun.
>
> 'Now what's that for?' cried Seaman Dick,
>
> Says I, 'Blow high, blow low,
>
> We'll give the lubbers one more kick!'
>
> Yo ho, and the rum below!"

"They seem contented enough now," said the skipper.
"I'll see those men, and then snatch a wink of sleep while
Mr. Newgate takes the watch." And he looked at me kindly.
"If you want to take a walk, young man, you may."

I know that I blushed, but when I looked at Gwendolyn
she was eying me quite calmly. She seemed, indeed, to be
faintly amused at my evident embarrassment.

"I'm not particularly interested in watching *that*," she

said, nodding at the carousing figures around the distant fires. "And so I'd as leave take your arm, sir."

So we left the skipper's fire, and found a sheltered spot in the edge of the trees, some distance to south'ard of the convict ship's dark bows.

While I was all eagerness and plied her with a myriad questions, she was a very contained, calm girl that night, though now and again I felt her dark eyes slyly inspecting my profile, and occasionally saw her smile.

Her low voice thrilled me. This I made no attempt to hide; but as the minutes sped away, and we talked of Virginia, the night's attack, our chances of freedom, and what not, she continually shunted me away from personalities. And this so nettled me that finally I fell into a glum silence.

"Come!" she chuckled. "You're thinking that I'm ungrateful, perhaps, because I don't fall on your neck in return for your kindness. Well—"

"Kindness?" I cried. My eyes blazed my delight in the soft curves of her smooth cheeks, the exquisite lips, the dark, intelligent eyes, the thick, wavy tresses that held such alluring lights and intoxicated me with their subtle perfume. "It wasn't just kindness I was showing you!" I exploded. "Why, from the moment I saw you—"

"Please don't!" she interrupted.

"You mean there is something else?" I cried.

She laughed low. "No," she returned. "I'm just not keen over wearing the ball and chain your sex expects mine to put on. You're an impulsive, generous soul, Ned Allen, and you've seen me in a situation that would—well, rather color things for you. And honestly"—she smiled teasingly—"you'll find, for one thing, that I've a deucedly rotten temper."

"I'd risk it," I promptly assured her.

But she shook her head, and at the same time was smiling provokingly at me from under her long lashes, when we heard some one approaching. It was still dark, though daylight was drawing near, and I did not recognize the man till he called in a low, cautious voice:

"Hey, Ned Allen? Are you there, Ned?"

It was old Tom Newgate.

I answered him, and he hurried to us.

"I've got to speak," he panted, wiping nervously at his broad face, which was perspiring with fear or excitement. "And Tiger Dick mought suspect suthin' if I was to wake the cap'n and take him aside. It's you as will have to tell Cap'n Fogg as there's murder afoot, and worse."

The deadly chill of terror laid a cold and heavy hand upon my heart. My voice sounded strained and unnatural as I cried in a low tone:

"You mean there's mutiny afoot, because of that treasure yarn?"

"It ain't no yarn, but plain fact—worse luck!" he hoarsely assured me.

"What?" I gasped. "There's treasure here?"

"There is, and no mistake! It's Tiger Dick and them swabs as I once sailed with on the old pirate ship *Typhoon* as means to get it, too. They aims to slash every honest throat and put to sea with the blunt!"

# 12

## THE PIRATE PLOT

**THE STUNNING NEWS** nearly floored me, but I was forced to rally; time was passing. "Do they mean to strike to-night?" I demanded.

"No," he said; at which Gwendolyn and I breathed somewhat easier. "Dick means to wait till all are on board. He don't want none to escape here on the island."

"So my impressions were correct!" I could not help but gasp excitedly. "Bellew and his messmates were pirates, and this abominable rogue was their mate—"

"Mate?" old Tom interrupted, snorting. "That man a mate? That man were born a capting, that he were! Cap'n of the old *Typhoon*, was Tiger Dick—and Jed Morgan were his mate. I were bo's'n. Aye, and Long Tom Bellew were quartermaster, and Horse Andrews cox'n. Ah, but if that old ship out there on the reef could talk, she'd tell you tales that would sizzle your hair at the roots, by thunder!"

"You mean that's the pirate ship *Typhoon*, wrecked there on the coral reef off Cutlass Sprit below this bay?"

"The same as ever was. Well did I know she was there, even afore I seed her this trip."

"That's what you wanted to tell me, Tom?" I cried.

"It were, son, only I couldn't make up my mind to peach.

Now here's the story: Nigh onto a year ago, it were, we lay off Trinidad. Jed Morgan and Dick was ashore. Along about four bells o' the morning watch here comes Jed aboard ship, and looking mighty pale about the gills. Says he to Long Tom, 'Some one knifed the cap'n. I finds him in an alley, and he's in hospital, a dyin'.' That's the story he told us.

"Ashore we goes—Long Tom, Horse Andrews, Hardy Flintlock and the dwarf Bruno along of me. I seed Dick with my own eyes, there in hospital, and if ever a man had the death haul on him, it were Dick. The doctor swabs they tells us no man was ever cut up like him and lived. He'd be dead afore two hours, they said.

"I've seen the scars," I interjected.

"Aye, the devil himself couldn't have lived with them cuts. Well, there was a prize we'd heard of, and we was anxious for to put to sea. So we leaves Bruno with him, and doubloons aplenty for to bury him all proper and ship-shape. What more could we do for him, says you? And we puts to sea, after putting up Jed for cap'n. We didn't know then as it were Jed who had stabbed him in the back, d'you see?"

"We took that prize, and two more, netting us over four hundred thousand pounds. But our luck had run its course. We starts to put into this here bay to careen and scrape, when up comes the wind to blow blue guns and piles us on that reef. Only fourteen of us got off alive.

"That's how come we spaded under that blunt. We hadn't no boat big enough to lug it away. Lucky we were to have saved the longboat to get off in ourselves. Come calm weather, we unloaded the blunt and what else we could save, and takes the whole ashore. After burying the stuff, we decides to put to sea.

"Picked up, we were, by a Frenchman, and finally makes Bristol. We'd 'a' taken that there Frenchman, only she was a man-o'-war. Well, then we needed a ship. We'd brought along enough to get a small sloop, and was smugglin', with an eye to windward, lookin' for a chance to steal a good schooner, when we has dirty luck again. All but Jed and me was aboard the night they got catched by them revenooers. That ended our smuggling operations.

"It was while our mates was a waitin' for trial that we hears Dick didn't die. Then Jed's uncle left him that there public house, and our mates was sentenced to Botany Bay. Which is how the convict ship, the *Vulture*, came here. Long Tom and his fellows put it up to that there Cap'n Bradbury to split with him if he'd let them off from goin' to Botany Bay, and he agreed to split and let 'em jump ship in Buenos Aires. Only, the *Bonny Lee* hove to in the offing, and that changed everything."

**THE SIGNIFICANCE OF** past events was now made plain to me. Dick had urged Camano Island as a splendid place to calk the *Bonny Lee's* seams because Tom Newgate had given his old captain the location of the cache; and once we should have repaired the leak, Dick, Tom and Bruno had proposed to murder the other four of us in our sleep!

But after the appearance of Long Tom and his eleven shipmates aboard the *Vulture*, Dick had struck a bargain with the other buccaneers, who agreed to throw over Bradbury's clique, while Dick inveigled us into a scheme which was ultimately to lead us straight to our own destruction! The scheming Bradbury had all unwittingly aided Dick

*"We took that prize"*

in gaining Cap'n Fogg's aid; for Bradbury's seizure of the *Bonny Lee* was actuated by a desire to shunt aboard the schooner all the sailors, soldiers and convicts that he could be conveniently rid of, thus reducing the number aboard the *Vulture* whom he must contend with in case of possible trouble over the money.

"Once afloat, you see," said Tom, "Bradbury meant to give the *Bonny Lee* the slip. But now we'd better budge. You warn the cap'n."

"What leads you to tell me this, Tom?" I took time to inquire as we started back through the trees.

He looked away toward Tops'l Hill, the majestic tip of which was still silvered by the sinking moon.

"A change has been a comin' over me!" he cried hoarsely. "I'm sick of it all. This blunt would do me no good. It's thousands I've had before, and who got it? Innkeepers and worse. A little shop—that's what I wants. It don't lead nowhere but to beggin' or a hornpipe at a rope's end, this don't. And that man—that Cap'n Fogg—I never saw a better man. Why, when he trusted me—say, that touched somethin' in my heart as I thought were dead these many years gone!"

"You'll never regret warning us, if we pull through!" I fervently assured him.

I had scarcely spoken when Gwendolyn—who had not uttered one word since Tom came up—suddenly grasped my hand.

A party of men were coming toward us on the beach. **THEY HAD NOT** sighted us, for we were well within the trees. Instantly we crouched down.

"It's Dick," old Tom warned us in a whisper.

We waited breathlessly, while the low hum of earnest voices grew momentarily louder. Not far from us they halted. Though I could discern no feature clearly, I recognized Dick, Long Tom Bellew, Hardy Flintlock, and that one of the O'Shaughnessy brothers who had survived the unmerciful, brutal beating administered on the *Vulture*.

It was to O'Shaughnessy that Dick was speaking.

"Man," he was saying, beseechingly, in his wonderfully deep and honeyed voice, "we've brought you here to save your skin, by thunder! What you do won't noways make any difference, save to yourself. Free to join, you are, or say no, as far as I'm concerned. But do you mean to tell me that you, with your own brother as dead as bilge—God rest his soul!—and your own body so sore as a boil, that you'll hang in stays?"

"It was not Captain Fogg and his men that killed my brother!"

"I don't say no to that, do I? The point for you is this: the best Cap'n Fogg can do for you is to set you somewhere ashore in the colonies. Well, now, suppose war isn't declared? We have made ourselves pirates, whether or no. Some fool will blab, and you may lay to it. Then a Tory gets a-hold of it, and where will we be? No, mate. Join on with us, and it's a man's free life you'll lead, and a lot of brisk lads at your side when they tries to lay us by the heels."

"No!" O'Shaughnessy vehemently declared. "What you propose is monstrous villainy. I'd no more take part in it than I would cut my own mother's throat."

"Is that your last word?" Dick inquired, his voice as soft as silk.

"That's my last word. I'll have nothing to do with you."

Dick's answer came in the form of a movement so swift that my eye could hardly follow the stroke. His heavy knife blade must have cleaved with the speed of light straight through O'Shaughnessy's breastbone and into the heart. The victim never cried out.

One thing kept me from firing upon the monster, who now chuckled and withdrew his blade from the corpse. This was the knowledge that I might miss, and that, even if I killed him, the shot would doubtless result in an immediate uprising that would in all likelihood prevent us from regaining the ship, even though we had all the firearms.

"Scoop out a hole and stow him," said Tiger Dick, quite calmly.

# 13

## BETWEEN TWO FIRES

**WE WAITED TILL** the murderers were well away before we dared to move. Gwendolyn sat tense beside me, her hand as cold as ice. Old Tom, however, seemed even more deeply affected than she, for Dick and his mates were hardly beyond earshot when he gripped his grizzled head in his broad hands and rocked to and fro.

"God ha' mercy on me!" he moaned. "It's me as got Dick aboard the *Bonny Lee* and told him of the blunt. Ah, but I've a deal to answer for!"

"You're doing your best to make up for the past," Gwendolyn kindly assured him.

"Ah, but it's a poor best, it is, m' lady."

"Spilled milk," I said, springing up. "Let's budge."

We suited the action to the word, Tom separating from us and taking another route by way of caution. The captain must be told of this at once.

Dick was talking to the skipper when we approached, but left before we came up, and went to the other end of the camp. The first streaks of day were showing in the sky, and most of the buccaneers at the other fire had succumbed to rum and slumber. They lay sprawled on the sands in ugly, sodden postures, their red mouths gaping, their new sailor togs befouled and bedraggled. Meanwhile, six of the released convicts were near the skipper—five asleep and one on guard.

The captain had roused and was filling a pipe, when we came up.

"Captain," I said at once, "the worst has come to pass."

His hand stopped dead midway between pouch and pipe bowl. Tom Newgate joined us when I was part way through my brief story, but the skipper remained motionless, never removing his eyes from mine to the end.

"A man to reckon with is yon Tiger Dick," was his only comment. Briskly he filled his pipe, and secured a taper from the fire. His hand trembled a little while he lighted the fragrant tobacco. Then said he: "We'll make ready to go aboard."

"Have you a word of forgiveness for such as me, sir?" old Tom pleaded.

"I'm not your judge for what you have done in the past. Insofar as I'm concerned, though, that's wiped out by the service you've given to-night."

"Ah, thankee kindly, sir," said old Tom.

Quietly we awakened the rest of the six new hands—landsmen, every one. Briefly the skipper acquainted them with our grave situation. They grew pallid and tight-lipped at the news, but not one of them flinched. Gwendolyn had chosen her men well.

"I think, sir," said one quiet chap named Cairnes, "that I speak for all six of us when I say that we're with you to the end."

"Thank you," said the skipper. And he proceeded to outline his plan.

Daylight comes quickly in the tropics, and visibility had increased markedly by the time we had gathered the muskets. We could not see that any one was watching us from the other fires. Only four or five men being still awake there, and these reeling drunk, we were enabled to dispose of the muskets without arousing the mutineers. Two were to be carried by each man to the gig. The others we quietly choked with sand.

"I'd take those other women," the skipper said, when we were ready, "but they threw in their lot with their kind last night, and I can't see that they rate the risk of waiting. Step out, now, lads!"

**AT THE DOUBLE** we ran down toward the gigs. Immediately one of the drunken brutes at the buccaneers' fire stumbled up with an oath; but this only served to quicken our pace.

By the time we reached the gig, several mutineers were on their feet. They shouted drunkenly at their sleeping comrades. Dick appeared at the edge of the trees, shouting words which we could not catch. But when Cap'n Fogg paused and fired a shot at them, the majority of the rascals stampeded for cover.

A few strokes of the ax put the other boats out of the running, and we then embarked and started rowing for the *Bonny Lee.*

The *Bonny Lee* was lying about three hundred yards off shore, and two hundred yards or more to southeastward of the beached *Vulture.* And the men at the oars were inexperienced and unable to hold to that well-timed swing and recover which makes for speed in rowing.

To make matters worse, we had not covered more than a

quarter of the distance before we saw Dick leading his men toward the *Vulture*. Up the ladders they ran like monkeys. In a trice some of them were busy tearing the canvas jacket off one of the long toms.

The captain and I were in the sheets. The loaded muskets had been passed to me, and I was watching astern.

"Captain," said I, "see what's toward."

He looked back over his shoulder.

"Damn!" said he. "Well, we can't stop now. Mr. Allen, you'd best begin firing."

I promptly complied, and though the boat was unsteady, had the satisfaction of seeing the splinters fly from the *Vulture's* bulwarks. It served to scatter the fellows around the gun.

Next I heard Dick roaring curses, and he jumped to the gun in person. My second shot I aimed directly at him. But the boat was again unsteady and my bullet whistled over his head.

Following his example, the buccaneers rallied, some leaping to aid Dick, and some appearing on deck with muskets in their hands. These fresh firearms they set to loading with all haste.

"Watch for the match, and I'll change course," said Cap'n Fogg.

Drunk though they were, the buccaneers were making quick work of loading. As steadily as I could I aimed first one musket, and then another. Luck was against me, though; I missed Dick, and nicked the shoulder of a ruffian beside him. The others thrust him aside and ran the piece forward on its carriage.

"The match, sir!" cried Tom Newgate, from the bow.

"Pull, my hearties!" roared the skipper.

We had been making straight away from the *Vulture*, and lay almost stern on to the buccaneers. Now the skipper laid the helm hard a-starboard.

Almost immediately afterward we heard the roar of the gun's report, and saw the great cloud of smoke belch from the *Vulture's* side.

There was a crash forward; the gig shivered from stem to stern; and a great fountain of water shot high into the air, just off our bow. I looked forward, past the white faces of our panic-stricken crew, and saw the extent of our damage. The round shot had struck the decked-over bow, smashing through this upper structure, and plunging out through a jagged hole in the sheer strake. While the hole was above the water line, we dared not list to port for fear of swamping.

"Steady, all!" Cap'n Fogg cried out. Every one had stopped rowing, thinking that we were going down. "We'll make it if we sit tight, my lads. Steady, all—give way!"

**THE VERY CALMNESS** of the man brought all out of their panic. Once more we were under way, striving mightily to pass round the *Bonny Lee's* stern before the murderous rascals on the black *Vulture* could fire another round shot.

We were not to escape thus easily, it proved. The buccaneers with the muskets had finished loading. One after another blazed away at us over the bulwarks, in a sort of ragged volley; and one musket ball crashed through the stern planking and wounded Cap'n Fogg in the leg. The shock doubled him over in agony before he could recover.

"You'll—have to—take the helm," he gasped at me, growing very pale and weaving on his seat.

I sprang to the helm and supported the fainting captain; and then, to our dismay, a hubbub broke out on the *Bonny Lee.* Abe Kemp ran across the deck as though pursued by devils and dived overboard. Behind him swarmed a horde of cursing British soldiers and seamen, with Tyron in the lead!

The *Vulture's* crew, prisoners in the hold but a short time before, were now in full control of the *Bonny Lee.* We in the gig were assuredly caught between the devil and the deep sea.

So disconcerted were we that all ceased rowing, not knowing what to do.

"Mr. Allen," groaned old Tom, "I reckon we're sunk."

"No, no!" cried Gwendolyn. "We can get astern and then pull for shore."

I saw what she meant. We were not more than a hundred yards from the *Bonny Lee.* She lay nearly broadside on to the *Vulture.* Our best chance lay in steering so as to come in astern of her, for then they could not bring the brass cannon to bear on us.

"Give way, all!" I shouted, shoving over the helm. "It's our only chance."

A Britisher at the rail fired a pistol at Abe Kemp, whose head appeared above the water. The bullet chugged into the water within a foot of the brave swimmer. Instantly he went under again, and Tyron barked out a command to his men to hold their fire, and hailed us.

"Come aboard!" he called, his voice carrying easily over the water. "If you do, I'll prefer no charges against any of you for piracy."

"That's because it's you he wants!" old Tom cried,

addressing Gwendolyn. "Well, he can go hang. I'll not take immunity for no such price, not I."

"Nor I!" seconded one of the men at the oars.

"Bring her safe aboard and escape the rope!" Tyron called through cupped hands.

He received his answer from Gwendolyn. "I'd rather be drowned than live on the same deck with you!" she cried.

Her words wounded him more severely than lead might have done. Raging and cursing, he fell upon his men with swinging fists.

"Get loaded before they are clear astern!" he roared. "Move, you scum! Have you nothing but feet at the end of your arms?"

This, in its way, only served to aid us. Each stroke of the oars brought us closer to the land we sought, and Tyron's crew had not finished priming the first piece, and I was thinking that surely we would make it when Gwendolyn exclaimed, "Behind you, Ned! The match!"

I looked over my shoulder, and saw the buccaneers training a gun upon us.

"Give way!" I cried, jamming over the helm.

WE WERE A bit too late. The sizzling projectile churned the water just astern of us, passing close under our keel, and throwing a fountain of spray high into the air. A sheet of water pelted me in the back, and filled the gig to the depth of a foot.

That catastrophe was well-nigh the end of us. Those facing the *Vulture* had also been slapped squarely in the face by the flying water, and were gasping for breath. Two dropped their oars, and, in reaching for them, nearly upset the gig. One oar was retrieved, but the other floated out of reach; and before Tom Newgate and I could calm the rest, we had shipped more water over the side.

"Bail with your caps!" cried Tom. "It's our one chance."

A few of us set to, but some sat as though numbed, while a half dozen men led by Tyron came running to the poop of the *Bonny Lee*. They had finished loading some of the muskets taken from that cargo in the vessel's hold.

"Will you bring that girl aboard now?" yelled Tyron.

"I'd brain the first man as pulled an oar toward you!" old Tom retorted.

"Aim at the men and let 'em have it!" Tyron hoarsely commanded.

Six men fired at us, and one bullet landed within an inch of Gwendolyn's hand. A second bit of lead knocked Tom Newgate's cap from his head, while still another passed below the water line and punctured the hull.

"I can't have you all killed like this!" wailed Gwendolyn. "I'd better—"

"Belay that!" thundered old Tom, plugging the hole with kerchiefs. "Mr. Allen, where's your head? Keep those lads bailing."

It served to rouse us to even more feverish efforts, but our case appeared hopeless. Another volley would surely find human targets, or sink us.

I was thinking this, and bailing with half an eye on the distance to shore, when from the side of the beached *Vulture* there billowed three clouds of smoke. Dick's buccaneers had trained the remaining three guns of the *Vulture's* port side battery upon the anchored schooner. The three eighteen-pounders struck the floating ship with a crash that shook her from truck to keelson.

# 14

## THE BATTLE IN HANGMAN'S BAY

**CONSTERNATION REIGNED MOMENTARILY** aboard the *Bonny Lee,* for one shot had hit the schooner below the water line.

The men on the poop immediately ran below and were lost to sight. A moment later the nine-pounders belched flame and smoke, one shot smashing a hole in the *Vulture's* bulwarks, while a second punctured the woodwork just below.

"Heads up, my hearties!" warned old Tom. "That there might be the saving of us, but the Lord helps them as helps themselves, by thunder!"

We fell furiously to bailing, our courage renewed. If the Britishers aboard the schooner could succeed in plugging the hole, and the *Bonny Lee* did not swing off, the buccaneers might find their hands so full that we could reach the safety of shore.

But our hopes in this quarter were dashed. We heard men crying out within the *Bonny Lee's* hold, and in a moment others ran forward to slip her cable.

We were barely under way toward shore when she began drifting rapidly toward the southern end of the harbor.

Tyron in the meantime was driving on his crew with furious curses, to put boats over the side.

"One of them sailors has told him about the spit this side o' the harbor!" cried old Tom. "They'll race to beach her afore she sinks."

Left to her own devices, the *Bonny Lee* would undoubtedly have been carried by the current into midchannel. Had she sunk there, all hopes of refloating her would have vanished. On the other hand, if she could be grounded on the spit, in shallow water, Tyron's men might patch the gap at low tide.

Thus a sort of three-cornered race took place, the pirates working in a frenzy of haste to sink the *Bonny Lee* or her boats, the Britishers to ground their schooner on the spit, and we to reach shore and the temporary safety of the trees.

Never has a shore appeared so unattainable to me. It seemed that we barely crawled, while now, in place of having only our stern exposed to the murderous rascals on the *Vulture*, our whole length lay at right angles to their line of fire.

"If they miss this time it's a miracle," said Cap'n Fogg, rousing out of a semi-coma at this moment.

"A few more boat lengths and we can wade!" cried old Tom.

This was heartening, and another circumstance aided us. The buccaneers did not fire. Dick doubtless reasoned that he had ample time in which to sink us before we put in.

"It's the two gigs of the *Bonny Lee* he hopes for a shot at, thank God!" exclaimed one of our crew.

**TYRON'S MEN WERE** oversides with their boats by then, taking good care to keep the schooner between themselves and the *Vulture's* guns. Some of those on deck had tossed a line to the boat crews from the bow, and against this they heaved in tandem, rowing desperately to bring the schooner's bowsprit round to southward.

The filling schooner held back like a stubborn mule. A capricious twist of the current jerked her bow up to northward, bringing the nearest boat into view of the buccaneers. The pirates yelled in glee; the Britishers rowed like madmen; but before the latter could start the bow round, three of the *Vulture's* guns had fired, one after the other.

None of the three shots hit either of the British gigs directly, though the one nearest the bow was partially filled with spray. Some of the men began bailing while the remainder still pulled at the oars. And suddenly the current released the *Bonny Lee*. She paid off and swung her stern toward the *Vulture*, putting her bulk between the two boats and the buccaneers.

"What may be the saving o' them may mean the long shore for us!" cried old Tom. "Look!"

As he spoke, the buccaneers fired their remaining piece full at us, and the shot plowed into the water close to the boat, ripping out a section of the keel. Spray blinded us; and in a trice all of our hapless crew were struggling in water up to the armpits.

Puffing and blowing like porpoises, we snatched for the damp muskets and started wading frantically toward shore, two of us assisting our wounded captain.

At every step the water seemed to take delight in holding back my eager feet. And I had not taken more than a dozen when I saw a half dozen ruffians leap from the deck of the *Vulture* to the sands and start running along the beach to cut us off!

"The reef, lads, the reef!" called out Cap'n Fogg. "We'll lay to there."

Not more than thirty yards from me was a short coral reef which projected about three feet above the surface of the bay. It was shaped somewhat like a half moon, so that he who knelt close to it was screened from the view of the pirates on the *Vulture* as well as those coming along the shore.

We plunged forward toward this, and the murderers upon the beach saw what we intended. One after the other paused and fired a pistol at us. The balls chugged into the water all around us, and Nate Crow, one of our new hands, fell shot through the head.

Half stumbling, half falling, the rest of us came to our knees in the shallow water while the running buccaneers were still midway between the convict ship and the trees just opposite our white ridge of coral.

I WAS SO blinded by perspiration, and so spent that things blurred before me, and I could only sob for breath. When my eyes cleared I saw that all our party save Abe Kemp had gained the refuge. This brave fellow had kept up a steady sailor's breast stroke behind us till he could touch bottom, and now came wading to us.

"It were that skunk of a Fallon—that convict we trusted—as sold us out to that Beau Tyron," he briefly explained. "Managed to turn 'em loose in the hold, he did. They've got Jerry Coffin a prisoner, but I was more spry, I guess. Has any one here a dry musket, by any chance? I wants a crack at them swabs, I do."

"Dry muskets?" cried the skipper. He had regained his breath, though I could see that he kept himself from fainting by sheer, dogged will power. "We must not hang in stays, lads," he went on. "Search yourselves for dry rags, and lively."

Search as we would, we could muster but a few small bits of dry cloth: Three of the powder horns had not leaked, but all the muskets and pistols had been immersed. We first fell to on those discharged while I was firing at the *Vulture,* striving to dry the barrels while others worked to draw the damp charges from those still loaded.

Horse Andrews and his five pirates were now opposite us, on shore. They were busy reloading their pistols, and keeping close to the trees.

"Was it gentlemen o' fortune you set out to be?" Horse Andrews scoffed at them. "Don't you go for to get too far from that there tree, Slim, or that girl will throw a rock at you."

"Aw, well, if you're so brash, go on and wade out to 'em!" growled the man called Slim.

"Right you are," said another. "Why, the tide'll get 'em, if we waits long enough."

"Is that so?" cried Andrews—a tall, wide-shouldered villain, with eyes as yellow as a cat's. "Well, since you're better sea lawyers than fighters, what do you make o' that?"

He pointed to southward. At a point several hundred yards off, there jutted out from shore a long projection, formed partly of coral, and partly of sand, which at some places appeared above the surface of the harbor, and at others lay submerged to a depth not exceeding four fathoms.

As I looked, the *Bonny Lee* grounded upon this, and swung slowly round till her starboard side lay almost parallel to the *Vulture.*

She had no more than struck when the men in the boats cheered, cast off the line, and started rowing ashore.

"See that?" cried Andrews. "That Tyron aims to pick off our hands from behind the trees, as like as not, once they're within musket shot. Now, I've had enough o' this palaver, I has. Out there is a passel o' half-drowned rats as may come to life again if we don't act before we has tougher than them to deal with. If hucksters ain't your size, you'll follow me!"

And with a deep chested roar he started into the water at a run. His mates, with a chorus of yells, came thundering after.

# 15

## SAFETY LIES IN BOLDNESS

**ALL OF US** popped up at this to be ready for them. We had cutlasses, to be sure, but of all the muskets there were only three which we hoped would be dry enough to fire. Abe Kemp, Tom Newgate and I gripped these pieces, while the convicts, Wheaton, Cairnes, Digby, Traynor and Mullins, had only sabers and wet rifles.

"You lads with the good muskets hold your fire till they're close in," the skipper ordered. "Mr. Newgate, take that man Andrews. Mr. Allen, the fellow with the red bandanna. Kemp, the man with the yellow sash."

He had ample time for these cool directions, for once the six buccaneers were in the water their pace slowed.

"You said them muskets was all wet!" cried one of the pirates, lagging behind. And he whipped up his pistol and fired.

All the others save Andrews immediately followed suit, the pistol balls chugging into the coral reef before us, or passing between us.

"You should have waited, you fools!" roared Andrews. "Never mind those muskets—they're only bluffing."

By this time they were halfway between shore and reef, and the skipper spoke up. "Take good aim and fire now, my lads," said he.

I pulled trigger, but nothing came of it save a click. The priming was damp. It sickened me to hear Tom Newgate's hammer fall with similar results. Abe Kemp was the only one of the three whose trigger finger sent a leaden slug across that stretch of shallow water.

The man with the yellow sash stumbled, clutched at his breast, and slumped with a sodden splash into the water. There he threshed like a hooked fish, in a lather of foam and blood.

This man's fall stopped the pirates in their tracks. At the same time one of them shouted hoarsely: "See there, Horse—the redcoats!"

"We'll be caught atween two fires, Horse!" the fellow with the red bandanna protested.

"Up, lads, and at 'em!" cried Cap'n Fogg, before Horse could reply.

All the men in our party leaped up. To remain on the reef meant that Tyron's men would soon be between us and safety; when the tide came up to flood we must either surrender or drown like rats; and with this staring us in the face we clubbed our weapons and surged over the reef.

The buccaneers broke before us. Not a one of them even paused to look at their fallen comrade. Horse Andrews made haste to overtake his mates. Not till he had reached the sandy beach did he pause. His men were already running toward the *Vulture*.

"I'll settle accounts with you, anyway, for a soft-bellied turncoat!" he panted, aiming his pistol full at Tom Newgate.

The pistol was not discharged. Cooler than most of us, Abe Kemp had waded along quietly, reloading as he came.

Now he threw up his musket and fired. Andrews spun and pitched to the sands, quite dead.

**THE BOATLOAD OF** British tars under Tyron appeared just then from behind a hummock to southward. They started immediately toward us, on the sandy beach, while to northward, upon the deck of the *Vulture,* we heard the buccaneers shouting derisively at their four comrades— who were still running for safety. Tiger Dick was scrambling down a ladder to the sands, followed by a dozen or more pirates.

We saw that we were about to be caught between the jaws of a vise. Hence we called on all our remaining strength and, once upon firm footing, made all haste possible in getting out of sight within the trees.

Abe Kemp picked the skipper up in his arms, as one might have handled a doll, and trotted off with him. In this manner we were soon shielded from view of the enemies behind us, the thick ferns affording a natural screen; but by the trail we left in pushing through them we knew that the poorest of trackers would have no difficulty in following.

"Easy all!" Tom Newgate said presently, holding up his hand. Behind us we heard muskets and pistols cracking, but no bullets flew near us. "They'll be having tea with one another for some time," he went on, panting for breath. "Well, now, I've an idea."

"We're listening, sir," said Abe Kemp. "Cap'n's fainted, so you're in command."

Old Tom looked round at our pale faces. "Here we are with no food, little powder, and starvation and worse a-facing us," said he. "Mayhap we can prolong our lives somewhat by playin' hide and seek, but I'm all for boldness, I am, in time o' need. There's one place I think is best, if we can make it."

"What place is that, sir?"

"Why, the blockhouse at the north end o' Hangman's Bay. It's there we stored most everything movable aboard the old *Typhoon.* All but the blunt, that is. There's powder there, and plenty guns, and—what's maybe a precious sight more important right now—there should be food."

"Let's get to the blockhouse, then," said Gwendolyn. "If there's a guard there, it can't be a large one."

There being no dissenting voice, old Tom set out at our head, wending northward.

There was no pursuit. By the sounds we judged that the buccaneers and their adversaries had scattered among the trees along the beach, where they were engaged in a sort of Indian skirmish. This continued till we had forded the creek and reached a high knoll from which we could see the *Vulture,* still upright on her props.

No men could now be seen on her deck, or upon the sands near by. To southward, grounded upon the spit, the *Bonny Lee* had heeled over on her port beams, her bow headed toward shore, her slant rendering the nine pounders useless to Tyron's soldiers.

Of the combatants we saw nothing, though the firing indicated that the majority were still bushwhacking at one another in the trees midway between the two ships. As for the blockhouse, we could discern no buccaneer within gunshot of it. Unless the guard was keeping out of sight within, our way seemed clear to food and a position where we could make a worthwhile stand in defense.

# 16

## A RASH FORAY

**TOM LED US** circuitously through the trees till we came to a point to northward of the palisade.

"Now," said Tom, "all the able men ready with cutlasses." Saying which, he spat upon his hands, and started into the clearing at a run.

The clearing was about seventy-five yards wide. We reached the palisade without a shot being fired at us. Swarming up and over it, we dropped inside. Nothing stirred within the blockhouse. A swift rush up a sandy slope brought us to the door, at the rear, and we saw that our precautions had been needless. The place was deserted.

The rectangular interior was some thirty feet in width and about forty-five in length. A double layer of logs, with two feet of earth between, formed the walls.

Suitable square portholes had been cut through these walls on all four sides, most of them for musketeers, but two for guns of larger caliber. Two old carronades were in place there still.

The structure sat on a knoll, with about fifty yards intervening between each of its four sides and the palisade; and from any one of the portholes a defender could see beyond the palisade and into the clearing beyond. On three sides, the woods flanked the edges of this clearing, while on the south you looked from the portholes directly across the paling to the sloping, sandy beach.

Kegs of gunpowder, boxes of muskets, and piles of cutlasses were in one corner. In another were casks of rum and wine.

At other parts of the great room they had stored salt pork, in barrels of brine: dried figs and grapes, in stout casks; and painted Dutch cheese, shaped like pumpkins or apples. Other makes of cheese had been stored in closed earthern jars; and to these were added ship's biscuit, preserved in jars that had been closed with sealing wax, and sacks of chocolate and vanilla.

I also saw rolls of blue Peruvian cotton, silver mounted pistols and rapiers, inlaid daggers, a box full of gold watches, many delicately constructed, bottles containing highly perfumed brandies, some masterly paintings, Indian blankets, jars of verdigris, tubes of bamboo, sealed with a blue gum—in which Tom said they had carried coffee—and a great number of sealed glass vials containing tobacco. What with the miscellany of ship's gear, the cooking utensils, the tarpaulins, and the chests of clothing, we had enough gear, it seemed, to clothe a crew and found a ship.

We found the powder dry enough—thanks to the skill of some unknown cooper and the heavy thatching of the roof.

Three of our new hands were set at the task of loading muskets and pistols, and Tom and I hastened to take inventory of the food supply. We had enough coffee, chocolate, ship's biscuit and cheese to feed our party of ten mouths not more than a week.

**TOM ORDERED A** dram of grog all round, for a calker; and this restored some of our lost color. Then Gwendolyn volunteered to serve as cook; and a fire was laid in the old ship's stove, in one corner.

When the coffee was made, and breakfast over with, Gwendolyn had a tarpaulin stretched, in one corner. Several chests were stored there. Presently she came forth again. She had found no women's apparel, but had discarded the ugly prisoners' garb for silk breeches and ruffled shirt. A pretty sash was wrapped about her waist, and she pivoted slowly, hand on hip, saucily inviting me to note the effect.

"Would I not make a fine beau gallant?" her twinkling eyes seemed to say. And aloud she continued: "Better anything than those awful arrows. And if I'm to be ship's cook, this rig will keep the crew's mind off my cooking!"

It was then that the skipper suddenly sat up.

"Here," he cried, shaking his head, "what's all this? Where am I?"

We told him; and he ripped out an oath. "Me fainting! Will you give me the loan of those petticoats you've taken off, Miss Leigh? Mr. Newgate," he roared, "hand me a noggin o' rum, by hickory!"

Tom handed him a large bottle, holding a quart. The captain tipped it up, and swallowed fully a half of the contents.

"That," said he, smacking his lips, "is by way of a nip. In a minute or two I'll take a drink." He looked at his leg. The bullet had passed clean through, stopping its flight just under the skin. He reached into his pocket, opened his clasp knife, and—presto!—out flopped the bullet.

"Now," said he, "soak a bit of cloth in rum, some one, and wrap it round that leg—and you, Abe Kemp, fashion me a bit of a crutch, hand over hand. Then give me a hand up, for I've work to do."

Kemp, with a grin, hastened to knock together a crude crutch, whereupon the skipper lurched bravely to his feet. And when Tom had told him of the situation in greater detail, he shook his head.

"We're in a tight box, my lads, and no mistake," said he. "We must get more provisions."

"I've been thinking of that, sir," said I. "Well, by your leave, I think I see a way to get them."

"Speak up," said he.

**I POINTED OUT** through a porthole. Near the bows of the *Vulture* there still remained a pile of stores. I had concluded that all of the buccaneers were still engaged in the skirmish with Tyron's men, among the trees to southward of the *Vulture*.

"We can filch a load of supplies before they return, sir," said I.

"Bravo!" cried the skipper.

He immediately told off all the men save himself, Tom Newgate and Digby. And then, as the men tightened their belts, and looked to their pistols, Gwendolyn spoke up.

"I'm going, too," she announced.

"You are not!" I told her bluntly. She tossed her chin. "I can carry as much and run as fast as any one of you!" she declared.

"Let the men take the risks," said the skipper, shortly.

Gwendolyn subsided with a grimace at the captain, behind his back, and a frown at me as I led my foragers out of the blockhouse.

The six of us proceeded across the clearing to northward, keeping the blockhouse between us and the distant combatants; and, having crossed the palisade, we headed west through a clump of trees and into a long ravine to the south.

On either side of us the ravine rose to the height of twenty feet. A thick growth of trees, ferns and bushes flanked the upper edges. We had more than a hundred yards to go before we could come into the open space which sloped down to the beach and the *Vulture's* position.

Overhead the morning sun was mounting in a blue sky, clear of clouds. Within the confines of the valley the morning dew was rising in a thin mist, while the growing heat pressed down upon us oppressively. Perspiring freely, we hurried on at a dog trot, thinking to reach our goal before any of Tiger Dick's crew intercepted us; but we had not gone more than fifty yards when I sighted five fresh mounds of dirt before me in the ravine. From one of these hastily dug shallow graves, there protruded a heavy lock of a woman's brown hair!

Then, as we all stared, a voice above and behind us said:

"Let that man raise a pistol who thinks it's best for him!"

We all turned and there above us we saw a strapping, handsome, red-haired woman, togged like any buccaneer. Around her shapely waist was wound a bright blue sash; a black silk scarf was bound round her head; and in her capable hands she gripped two pistols.

"It's Belle Saunders!" gasped Mullins. "Don't move,

mates!" he hoarsely admonished us. "She was going to Botany Bay for life for shooting a cove on Wapping Heath, and she can knock a sov'ring out of your hand at twenty paces!"

"At thirty!" Belle corrected him in a throaty voice. Ah, but she was a swanking, confident figure as she stood there in her sea boots! She favored us with a contemptuous smile which displayed an even row of strong white teeth. A buxom, graceful, powerful woman, whom I had barely noticed in the hurly-burly of the previous night.

"At thirty paces," she went on, easily. "And this is only about fifteen. I'll be obliged," she continued, mockingly, "if every one of you will drop his pistols and cutlass at his feet."

**THERE WAS A** sickening situation! Not one of us wanted to kill a woman. Neither did we wish to risk the sound of the shots. Her pistols were double-barreled; we were of course certain that two or more of us would fall if we whirled and fired; but in our desperate situation it was not this danger which checked us for the moment. It was the fact that a woman confronted us that set the cold perspiration pouring down my spine, and kept me from giving the signal.

She read my thought readily. "I have you on the hip," she said, laughing. "Come, now—drop those weapons!"

But as the last word left her mouth, a lithe figure leaped like a catamount from the bushes behind her. Belle received a hard, square little shoulder full in the middle of her back; two strong arms clamped down her own; and the impact knocked her forward, and down the steep slope toward us. With her came Gwendolyn, clutching the larger woman's arms in a fierce grip.

Knocked completely off balance, Belle pitched headlong and face downward into the shifting sands of the slope, and Gwendolyn landed on her captive's back.

Belle was a strong woman, and would have succeeded in throwing Gwendolyn off in a moment had Abe and I not pinioned her arms so quickly. Disarmed and helpless, she relaxed, blew the sand from her red lips, and laughed mirthlessly.

"I diced and lost," said she. "Well, am I to hang, or roast upon a stake?"

Instead of answering I sent Abe Kemp aloft to scan the horizon; and as he ran up the bank, Gwendolyn eyed me saucily, demurely.

"Sorry I disobeyed and followed," said she. "But see what happened!"

"You needn't rub it in!" I snorted. "Abe, what's up?"

"About a half dozen swabs just below the *Vulture*," said he. "Headed south. Two sheets in the wind."

He crouched behind a bush. "They're going toward the trees, to south'ard. Reckon they're lugging back powder and shot."

I deemed it best to wait till they were well away before we advanced. So I turned to our prisoner.

"Who killed those five women?" I asked, nodding at the mounds.

"Who?" Belle exclaimed. "Why, that beastly little dwarf, Bruno. When the fighting started this morning, Dick sent orders for us girls to take cover, d'y'see. Next he sent that dwarf up the ravine to do the business—but I got away." Then she cried, her voice athrill with admiration, "I heard Dick say once, last night, 'Women? They're only more mouths to feed, and a source of trouble!' Ah, but there's a man for you, is Tiger Dick!"

"There's as big a monster as ever cheated gallows!" I told her indignantly.

She shrugged, and chuckled. "Life's but a battle, and devil take the hindmost. He'll not be hindmost, will Tiger Dick."

"The man who would have killed you, too!"

"Ah, well, he had had no chance to get well acquainted with me!" she said, saucily. "And that's what I was playing for, d'y'see."

"His favor, you mean?"

"Naught else," she stated brazenly. She spread her palms. "Maybe I could have joined you after I saw you'd got into the blockhouse. But you'll admit your chances looked mighty slim. They do yet, for that matter. Well—"

"So when we came along you thought you saw a chance to deliver us to Tiger Dick?"

"Certainly."

SHE EYED ME defiantly, and yet with so merry a smile that I nearly answered it. She was, in all truth, a magnetic woman, a woman of many charms. Her eyes were busily engaged, even then, in studying the faces round about her; and I noted that Mullins colored a bit and looked confused when he met her glance. At this Belle's long lashes dropped demurely, and she sighed.

"To think that you'd frown at me like that, Jeff Mullins!" she breathed, reproachfully.

"Me? Frown at you?" stammered Mullins, till indignation got the better of him. "Ah, if ever a fine smile hid a hard, flinty heart, it's yours." His sunken eyes burned in his gaunt, lean face as he towered over her.

"You always misunderstood me, Jeff," Belle returned sadly, still speaking with eyes downcast.

I saw that here was one of Fate's ghastly jokes. The man both loved and hated her. And I sensed that it was fear of his own weakness before her, as much as indignation, which caused him to speak so brusquely. It was pitiful.

"All this is neither here nor there," said I. I ordered the woman's arms to be bound behind her with kerchiefs, and said to Gwendolyn, "I suppose if I give you an order, you'll tell me to go hang. Will you condescend to take this prisoner back to Cap'n Fogg? This," I added, "is a *man's* job."

"Was it a man who captured Belle, forsooth?" she shot back at me—and went off with her prisoner, leaving me red about the ears.

"What's toward now, Abe?" I cried, brusquely, thinking to hide my confusion.

"Why," quoth Abe, from his observation point above me, "four of 'em stayed in camp, I see. They've come out from behind a tent, and are building a fire."

"Well," said I, "they're drunk, and we're six. Let's go."

With this we headed south toward the end of the ravine.

# 17

## THE RAID ON THE VULTURE

**BEYOND THE END** of the ravine was a hummock of sand which screened our approach from the four buccaneers at their fire. Once we reached it, I peered cautiously over the top.

The four rascals were but seventy-five yards distant. One I recognized as Joe Darby, wearing a red bandanna round his head. He was the only seasoned pirate there; the other three were recent remits from the landsmen among the convicts.

The gunfire to southward still continued, and from this I concluded that the majority of the buccaneers were so far removed from the fire that they could not return in time to block us from carrying away at least one load of supplies. Nor was this my only consideration. The starboard guns aboard the *Vulture* could be pointed at the blockhouse to support an attacking force.

"If we rout 'em, all but Abe and I are to grab what they can and leg it back to the stockade," said I. "Abe and I will cut the *Vulture's* props, and act as rear guard. Every one up beside me, now."

The men came up, their pistols ready. We carried two apiece. Only one, I directed, was to be fired by each man at this volley. The second pistol was to be held in reserve until we came to close quarters.

"Take aim!" I ordered. Then, when I was sure each man had a target, I cried, "Fire!"

The six heavy pistols boomed like so many small cannon.

It was long pistol range; but all six of our slugs ripped into the sand within a radius of ten feet of the fire.

Never were a sorry lot of villains more dumfounded. One made a frightened leap to southward, and ran straight down the beach with the speed of a man who thinks the devil himself is just behind him. The others were equally frightened, but one appeared blinded by sand, and Joe Darby stumbled over a mate in his rush, stretching both on the ground.

"At 'em, mates!" roared Abe Kemp. "Halve and quarter 'em—all-l-l hands!"

He had the lungs of a bull, had Abe, and his great voice followed close upon the volley like a clap of thunder. Spurred on by his thrilling roar, we were up and running like wild-eyed Vikings to the kill, our huzzahs pealing across the harbor, and our cutlasses whistling in the air.

This was enough for the remaining three pirates. Only Joe Darby fired at us, but his shot was delivered as he leaped up. The next breath saw him following the other two in a mad dash for the trees.

NONE OF US allowed grass to grow about our feet. We raced across the shallow creek to the camp, paused to reload, selected such small casks of pork and biscuits as could be conveniently carried, and started Mullins and his three comrades back toward the blockhouse. Then Abe and

I seized axes and ran for the starboard, or northern side of the *Vulture.*

The stern of the convict ship lay in about a foot of water, but the greater part of her rested on the dry sands. Deeply embedded in the sand were eight thick spars, set slantwise against the hull to prop her upright. Upon these Abe and I fell with furious strokes.

The spars were thick and tough. We chopped furiously, but the racing seconds were flying faster than the chips. When Abe severed the fourth and I was chopping at the fifth prop, shouts in the woods told me that the buccaneers were returning.

"Grab another keg and run, Abe!" I panted. "A few more strokes and the old girl will keel over—those three spars won't hold her."

Abe snatched up a small keg and ran with it under his arm. He paused, some distance away, as I severed the fifth prop. The big ship groaned and listed a bit, shoving the ends of the remaining three sticks deeper into the sands; but she had listed no more than a foot or two when she came to a dead stop.

"Let well enough alone!" Abe pleaded. "They're out on the beach—a dozen of 'em."

I had jumped back, and was whacking away at the sixth prop. "I'll have her down now," I cried, "if I have to stand off the lot of them!"

Abe's reply came in the form of two pistol shots which he fired at the approaching pirates. Not until then did he turn and run, calling back over his shoulder, "Leg it, you hot-headed kid!"

I had by this time nearly severed the stick. Another

stroke, I thought, would finish the business. I raised the ax; but suddenly the stick buckled, snapped with a sharp report, and the great hulk heeled over toward me.

I leaped backward, but I was not quick enough. The splintered end of that severed spar pierced through my trouser leg and pinned me fast as the dismasted hull crashed to the sand with a resounding thud.

Fortunately for me, the rounding contours of the *Vulture's* black hull kept her from coming clear over to a position flat upon her side. I was equally fortunate in that I was not opposite a gun port.

The four starboard guns buried their black snouts in the sand. Two of the port guns broke loose from their lashing, tumbled end over end, and crashed into the starboard bulwarks. One slithered over the breech of a starboard cannon, balanced an instant upon the bulwark, and tumbled to the sands. There it lay upon its black back, like a helpless beetle, within a yard of me.

The other gun smashed through the bulwark like a battering ram, coming to rest in a mess of wreckage. Roundshot, rammers, buckets and powder kegs piled atop her.

**PINNED THERE LIKE** a helpless calf upon a hook, my very terror served to aid me. My head cleared. I saw that I was merely pinned down by the tough canvas trousers, which ended just below my knees. I seized that strip of canvas in a grip enough to wrench a horse apart; one rip and I was free.

In a trice I was on my feet. I saw that Abe was fully a hundred yards or more on his way, but that he had paused to reload a pistol. Meanwhile the shouts of the buccaneers told me that some of them were not more than a few ship's lengths from the *Vulture's* bow.

To fly was out of the question for me; at that short range some of them would be fairly sure to drill me through the back; and I turned, in my extremity, and leaped over the bulwarks.

A more stupid man than Kemp might have revealed my presence to the pirates at that moment. But Abe raised his pistol, fired, picked up his keg, and ran on again toward the blockhouse. Thus he made it appear that he had paused solely to exchange shots with his pursuers.

A half dozen or more shots from the buccaneers answered him. Under cover of these reports I leaped for the edge of an open hatchway, caught it up with my hands, pulled myself up the slanting deck, and swung into the *Vulture's* hold.

Around the bow, in that same moment, came charging a cursing, roaring horde of drunken buccaneers.

# 18

## TRAPPED IN A WRECKED SHIP

**THE BLACK CONVICT** ship had been built with three decks—upper, main, and lower, or hold. I had dropped from the upper deck to a narrow passageway which bisected the main deck, fore and aft, between the lazaret (the storeroom which was under the main cabin astern) and the quarters forward. The fo'c's'le having been wedged between the bows, on the upper deck, space had been left below it, on the main deck, for the prisoners' berths, the soldiers' quarters, the galley and the locker room.

Except for the mischance of a lucky shot, I had little doubt that all of my party would make the stockade in safety. They had a long start, and the rum-fuddled pirates were but indifferent marksmen. Neither did I think that my mates could be overtaken. In a brace of shakes it was likely that the buccaneers would see the futility of pursuit, and return. By that time it would be best for me to be in a secure hiding-place.

The after part of the ship I discarded after but a second's thought. If it came to a siege, that would be too easy for my enemies to come at, by way of skylights, stern ports or companionway. Neither could I hope to overhear the cutthroats so easily from there. With this in mind, I started forward past the dark, foul-smelling convict cells, stepping as softly as though I were treading upon a carpet of eggs.

Reaching the locker room, I found the door to be unlocked. The door swung open when I leaned my shoulder against it. It was hinged on the port side, and I was careful to keep it from slamming after I had squeezed through.

Once inside, I dropped its bar in place. At least they could not come at me handily from the passageway! There was a ladder coming down from the fo'c's'le; but the hatch was closed, and I still had my two pistols. I was at least in a position, I reasoned, where I could sell my life dearly.

So securely was everything lashed or cleated that only a few odds and ends had fallen over against the canted starboard side when the ship fell. The open ports were free from wreckage, and I hopped to one of these.

The porthole was barely larger than a man's head, and I saw that it would not do as a means of escape, later. But it served well for the immediate purpose.

The firing had ceased. Away to the north I saw Abe Kemp, disappearing safely over the stockade. No wounded men lay on the slope; so I judged that Mullins and his three shipmates were already within the inclosure.

RETURNING AT A leisurely pace across the creek were a half dozen of the sweating buccaneers. Some were cursing, others were laughing recklessly. The others had paused near the fire, some sprawling on their broad backs, and three of them passing a bottle from hand to hand.

"Well, that's one to them!" one carelessly cried; and I recognized the hairy English sailor who had laid the whip so viciously upon my torn back! Near him were two other

*Ned Allen started forward past the*
*convict cells of the careened ship*

Britishers who had decided to sail under the Jolly Roger
rather than remain with Beau Tyron.

And I had just noted this disturbing fact when Tiger
Dick himself came into view. He was followed by a number
of his crew, and among them I saw two more English tars
who had been won over to the ranks of the buccaneers.

"Well, I reckon some o' you killed a goat or two on Tops'l
Hill!" said Dick, smiling sardonically. "Howsomever, the
damage is done. And now you see, mates, what comes o'
guzzle, guzzle, guzzle, afore the work is done—and letting
duty go hang."

"Well, what's the odds, cap'n?" roared one. "Give us a go
at that bottle, Joe Darby—and let's have a song all around."

"That's the way of it," said Dick contemptuously. "There
ain't more'n two or three mothers' sons o' you that has the
responsibility of a weevil. Here's some of you pan and left
Horse Andrews to get shot down like a dog—"

"Wasn't Tyron's men a comin'?"

"Suppose they were? We'd have been with you. Anyway,
you let Cap'n Fogg get ashore, after Tom Newgate turned

soft, and now see what's up! I sent you and your mates, Joe Darby, to hold that blockhouse, but you stopped here to take a calker. Now the blockhouse is gone, ship tipped over, supplies lifted—"

"But we thought it was some o' Tyron's men as had got round behind us!" Joe Darby protested.

"And anyway," said another, "we got all the best of it, cap'n. Thanks to your singin' out an offer to Tyron's men when we was scattered in the trees—why, we've got more mates than we had this mornin', by thunder!"

"Tyron can't get that there schooner afloat with us in the offing, either," declared Long Tom Bellew. "Come on and take a drink, Dick. You'll feel better."

Dick was looking hard at the ground near by, at the new masts.

"I don't need a drink as much as some sober hands!" he suddenly declared. "There ain't nary one of you four," he said to Joe Darby, "could tell me how many o' Fogg's hands laid you aboard. But I heard an ax, I did, when Abe Kemp and his four messmates was still in sight, running."

"Right you are!" gasped Long Tom. "By thunder, she was still on an even keel, and them swabs well away from her."

"Who took them last cuts, then?" bellowed Hardy.

"Some one that hasn't got away yet!" cried Dick. "Overhaul that craft, a dozen of ye—overhaul it alow and aloft."

**MY HEART POUNDED** heavily. I dropped noiselessly below the porthole, and for as much as a second or two stood weak and sick, my bones as soft as so much pulp. Then through my head flashed the thought that, if they found the door latched, the end would be but a question of time. Perhaps I could fool them for the time being. I sped to the

door, loosened the bar, whirled about, and sprang to the
ladder which led up to the fo'c's'le.

This was on the starboard side. Since the ship had heeled
in this direction, I had only to run up an easy incline to
reach the trapdoor. The door went up easily, and without
noise, and I popped into the fo'c's'le.

There was no hatchway in the deck above my head;
and the buccaneers could come at me only by forcing the
single door aft. By great good fortune this fo'c's'le door
was hinged to port, and so had swung tight shut. This shut
me off from view of the pirates. But I could hear them.
Some of the hardy rascals were already clambering over
the bulwarks on the ship's lower or starboard beam.

Then I saw a way out of this *cul-de-sac*. When the *Bonny
Lee* had fired at the *Vulture,* at fairly short range, before
Tyron's men cut the schooner adrift, the first nine-pounder
had bashed in the bulwarks of the *Vulture's* fo'c's'le. As the
ship lay now, there was the gaping hole, just above my head.

The jagged hole was at least three feet in diameter. On
either side of the fo'c's'le were triple rows of bunks; and the
nine-pound roundshot had plowed through the side, between
the middle and upper tier. I had only to hop up over one of
the bunks and pop out through the hole into the sunshine.

Lying there on the slanted side of the overturned ship
appealed to me as the least hazardous of the few moves
which grinning Fate had left to my hurried choice.

Presto! I had decided. I leaped at the bunk, and whipped
through the hole.

I had just moved to one side of it when Tiger Dick,
Bruno, and several buccaneers pushed open the fo'c's'le
door.

# 19

## HUNTED

**THE CANT OF** the *Vulture* had reduced the angle at which
her port side slanted to less than that of the average roof;
yet it was sufficient to hide me from the buccaneers who
remained at their breakfast fire. This blaze was burning
near the tarpaulins to north'ard, so that the hull intervened
between me and those around it. But would one or more of
them arise and walk southward to a position from which I
could be seen? That was a possibility to cut five years from
a man's life!

The ship was broad of beam; I was high above the sand,
and could not be seen by a man walking along the south
side of her, close to the hull; but the beach sloped upward,
the bow was headed inshore, and any buccaneer who
chanced to seek that point of observation would spot me
in a flash.

The prospect started the perspiration to flowing in
streams upon me. My thoughts were also engaged with
other possibilities. Would Tiger Dick think to stick his
head up through the hole I had just used? Would some
one think to look over the port bulwarks? And which had
I better watch—the hole or the bulwarks? I wished that
Nature could have been more generous in dealing out

eyes—for at that moment I needed a pair in the back of my head.

Within the fo'c's'le the buccaneers created a din, tossing out pallets, jerking sea chests from underneath the bunks, turning the quarters topsy-turvy. Yet no more than a minute could have passed before Tiger Dick cried:

"Well, if he's here, I'm blind. Lay below, my hearties!"

In a jiffy the searchers in the forward part of the ship had tumbled below, leaving the fo'c's'le deserted. Others were engaged in searching the after cabin and the lazaret. Now I heard an oath deep down in the hold; now they hallooed to one another to try this or that corner of the ship; and then suddenly I heard a man start to scramble up the slanting deck toward the port rail.

"Maybe the son of a rum puncheon hopped it over this side!" I heard him cry.

To leap down and run would give me but a few yards' start; so I determined on quite another course. I slipped back through the hole and into a seaman's bunk in the fo'c's'le.

"Well, Jack," I heard a pirate calling to the man who had apparently reached the upper bulwarks, "what do you see?"

"What Paddy shot at!" growled the man. Then he bellowed: "Hey, some o' you rum guzzlin' swabs, shake a leg! Maybe he's hiding under her bilge."

I heard some of the buccaneers leave the fire and come pounding round the port side, on the ground. But I was already moving. The cant of the craft had served to slam shut the fo'c's'le door once more, so none on deck could see me. For fear they might return and open that door I hastened stealthily into the chain room.

A high coil of three-inch hawser gave me my chance. I crouched down behind it, on the starboard side, and waited.

Within a minute I heard a yell from the buccaneers in the stern. Some of them had been chopping there, and now I heard them shouting that they had found a chest full of coins in the ship's strong room.

"Here's enough doubloons here, mates, to sink a jolly boat!" yelled one.

That ended the search. There was a scramble among the pirates to lay aft and view this new find.

In a moment or two I heard Dick ordering all back to the fire; and, peeking out the hawsehole, I saw them trudging by the ship, a brass bound chest carried by four brawny seamen, the whole crowd laughing and conjecturing like so many excited children.

"Well," Dick declared, "maybe Abe Kemp hit the last licks, and the prop cracked after he got away. But if that ain't it, and one of them gave us the slip, good luck to him, say I! Who's got the best of it, after all? Let's see the sun shining on those jolly dollars, mates!"

As they spread a canvas, and dumped the golden coins upon it, I thought, "Here's my chance, by thunder! I'll slip out now and run like a whitehead for the woods."

But Dick spoiled my chance. "They'll be sneaking up for a pot shot at us, if we don't look spry," said he. And he sent two of them down the beach to south'ard, to act as sentinels.

"That," I thought bitterly, "means that I will probably have to wait here until nightfall before I can get away!"

**THERE BEING NOTHING** else to do, I returned to the starboard hawsehole, from which I could watch the buccaneers counting their gold near the breakfast fire; and the total, it presently developed, amounted to ten thousand, two hundred and forty English pounds.

"Are you satisfied now to be a gentleman o' fortune?" Dick cried, when all had received a share, and some had fallen to dicing upon tarpaulins, spread smooth upon the sands.

"There's only one thing missing, sir," said a former *Vulture* hand.

"What's that?"

"I'd like to do a hornpipe with them women, so I would. Did they join up with Cap'n Fogg?"

"No," said Dick, chuckling dryly. "They're dancing on hot coals by now, I shouldn't wonder."

"What? You mean they're on the long shore?"

"I reckon they are!"

"Ah, but you were a bit stiff there, cap'n!" growled Long Tom Bellew, looking up from a dice game. "Them girls was jolly companions, one and all."

"Is that so, Tom Bellew?" Dick retorted, softly. He sat there at ease, upon an oaken cask, beneath a canvas awning. "Well," he continued, between puffs of his pipe, "how many times have I seen knives going, and friendships gone by the board, and a crew split into cliques, and all on account of chittering baggages without an ounce o' brains in their heads? When a cruise is done, and there's blunt safe in all fists, then let each man take his fancy and go hang, say I! But not when business is afore us. Just you forget the women till we're done with this cruise, my hearties!"

There were no further growls at this; and from their

subsequent talk I learned that the skirmish in the trees with Tyron's men had resulted in no deaths. Hampered by the thick foliage, and the drunken state of his men, Dick had been contented with stopping Tyron's crew from approaching the *Vulture*, and enticing several British tars to join his buccaneers.

"I'd have laid 'em by the board and taken the *Bonny Lee* if you men hadn't been two sheets in the wind's eye," said Dick.

An hour or more had passed when he said this. With the prodigality of their sort, the gamblers had wagered huge sums, and some were already as poor as they had been before the loot was divided. Long Tom Bellew was one of these.

"When do we lay them lubbers aboard?" he asked, surlily.

"When?" replied Dick. "Not afore the cool o' the afternoon, and the tide's right. Then we can wade right out that spit."

"Well, I don't say no to that, does I? But what I say is— why can't we go and dig up the rest o' our blunt?"

"Well, now, that blunt's safe where it is, I reckon. You ain't no more doubloons to gamble with, that's all that ails you, Tom. But we've business to attend to first."

Long Tom pointed out that Tom Newgate knew the location of the cache, which was under the lee of Tops'l Hill, not more than an eighth of a mile to north'ard of the block house. To this Dick retorted, "Cap'n Fogg has too few hands to risk a job like that, not knowing what we'd do."

He further contended that to weaken their forces by

sending a large enough party at this juncture to dig up the chests was inviting a disastrous attack by Beau Tyron.

"He'd set the old *Vulture* afire, like as not, and burn up our stores!" cried Dick. "Where'd we be then? Your head is addled with rum, Tom—go sleep it off, is my advice to you."

Even as Tom was turning away, one of the men shouted, "Why, sink me if that ain't Belle Saunders coming over that hummock!"

I STARED ACROSS the creek. True enough, there came Belle Saunders! She had escaped from—was it my party? The blood within me congealed as there weighed down upon me the sickening fear that she had, by hook or crook, overcome Gwendolyn before they reached the stockade!

Yet this seemed hardly possible. We had bound her arms behind her quite securely. Gwendolyn had carried two pistols. And then I guessed at the truth.

Knowing the fate meted out to her sisters on the preceding night, Belle would not have come running so boldly into the lion's den had she been without news of import. She had been safely guarded to the stockade, and then escaped.

Worse still, she must have known, from Abe Kemp and the others, that I had secreted myself within the hold of the *Vulture*. She had managed her escape, and was bringing this news straight to Dick!

The handsome woman, her hair flying, had breasted a sand hummock, across the creek.

There was nothing for me to do now but fly. I raced to the bunk, shot through the cannon ball hole, slid down the canted side of the old ship, and dropped to the sands.

I was running as I lit, so to speak. I headed straight

toward the trees, thinking that if I once gained cover I might escape the fusillade that was bound to follow me. But I had barely cleared the bows when pandemonium broke out among the buccaneers, and they were after me.

The island rang with the barks of a dozen pistols; all around about me the deadly missiles screeched and shrieked like so many vengeful demons. The fact that they had missed me thus far, and that those who fired the shots were drunk and excited, did not tend to lessen my terror.

Thinking that I would check them by returning the fire, I let fly with both pistols, the crack of one falling atop the other. But there I made a mistake. They were so close upon me that I kept on running, and did not pause to take steady aim. Consequently my shots missed. Worse still, a man cannot fire back over his shoulder, while running at full speed, and watch his feet. I tripped and fell.

"Now," the sickening thought came to me, "I'll get a knife in the back!"

But Dick had other plans.

"Stop firing!" he bellowed, in a thunderous voice. "Truss him up alive!"

An avalanche of human forms hurled me to the sands before I had reached my knees.

"Why not let 'er rip?" growled Hardy, as they jerked me to my feet.

"Stow that guff, Hardy," Dick retorted. He cast a glance at Belle Saunders, who had slowed to a walk. "I reckon you could trade that head for a painted dead-eye, Hardy. Why not cut him up? Why, because he's hostage—that's why."

# 20

## TREACHERY

**"HOSTAGE?" GASPED HARDY.** He chuckled, derisively. "For to keep them few lubbers in the stockade from harming us? Ho, ho!"

"Well, not exactly. First point: this man Allen is mighty sweet on that little wench in the stockade. Second point: I'll gamble that she'll come flying out of that there blockhouse afore she'd let us initiate him."

"Where does we profit there, though?" Long Tom asked, stupidly.

"Where? Well, now, maybe you fellows would rather gain an end by swingin' a cutlass than by compromise. Suppose she comes? What does that Beau Tyron come out from England on the *Vulture* for? Why, for that girl, that's what! Once we has her in hand, ain't we something to trade with?"

"Ah!" cried Long Tom Bellew, as the trend of this came home to him. "There's a prime dodge, and no mistake." He laughed uproariously. "Hats off to Tiger Dick, you swabs!" he yelled; and that crew of scoundrels, now that they saw the working of their leader's mind, grinned widely, one at the other, and sent up a cheer to split the heavens.

"So now you see," said Dick, smiling easily round about

him. "It's worth trying, anyway... Mr. Bellew," he added, with extravagant, sarcastic courtesy, "will you oblige me by ushering Mr. Allen into our midst?"

All this while he had remained as cool and collected as though he were sauntering along Piccadilly. Toward me he had barely so much as glanced. Now, as Long Tom and the others chuckled, he led the way back to the fire, his eyes taking in Belle's approaching figure.

"A lady to visit us," he said, musingly, sitting down on his upturned cask; and he began to fill his pipe, never taking his gaze from her.

I shall not soon forget the picture that she made. There was a brave, bold woman. She was dicing with Death, and she knew it, but upon her red lips was a provocative smile, and her eyes sparkled merrily, like twin jewels in her flushed, handsome face. One shapely hand rested easily upon her rounded hip, and she came forward with the graceful, insolent sway of a Spanish dancer, never looking at any one but Dick, never showing by as much as a sharp drawn breath the fear which must have lurked deep in her thumping heart.

"Well," said she, pausing before Dick at last, "I see I didn't come in vain."

"No," said Dick, smiling at her through narrowed eyes. "You didn't. Thankee for that." He shook his head slowly, looking her up and down. "You are a cool one, and no mistake," he added.

"Like yourself," she returned. She indicated the frowning Bruno with a careless, mocking nod. "You should have sent something better than an ape to finish *me*," she declared.

Dick laughed outright, clapping his thick thigh. "By

thunder, I didn't look closely at you last night!" he ejaculated—and a child might have seen that he was caught, hard and fast! The woman's beauty and boldness had struck an answering chord in that tigerish heart. He jumped up, and bowed low, sweeping his hat to the sands. "Here's my duty to you, ma'am, for one in a thousand!"

There was a horrible growl close by him. It came from the throat of the brute, Bruno. He saw himself being supplanted, as a faithful dog may be supplanted in a man's affection by the advent of a sweetheart, and green sparks danced in his red-rimmed eyes. Whipping out his knife, he hurled himself toward Belle.

The woman never moved. But Dick did. He wheeled, struck up the dwarf's hairy arm, and kicked the vicious little murderer fully twenty feet across the sands.

"Get busy, now," he ordered, when Bruno bounced up like a rubber ball, "and bring me a cask for the lady's seat."

There was a battle of looks between the two, but the scowling dwarf soon knuckled under, and, with no further parley, secured a cask and brought it surlily to Belle Saunders. She sat down gracefully beside Dick, smiling into his enamored eyes.

**"SO THAT'S THE** way of it!" said Hardy Flintlock. "What's sauce for the goose ain't sauce for the gander."

"Hardy," said Dick, as Bruno slunk into the background, "this here is different. I never see a woman like her, and I mean to marry her, all shipshape and regular, if she'll have me, by thunder! Is there any man here to say no to that?"

He turned from man to man, and no one spoke. Then he extended his hand toward Belle.

"Well?" he cried, eagerly.

The woman's eyes dropped, and from her bosom there spread upward a rich wave of crimson. Silently she placed her hand in his, concluding the strangest courtship it has ever been my lot to witness.

"We'll drink a noggin all round to that!" Dick happily declared; and when this was done he said, "Where have you been?"

She told him of her escape from Bruno, and her capture by my party. She had made no attempt to escape Gwendolyn on the way to the stockade. "But when the watch below was asleep," said she, "and the rest getting firewood, I saw my chance. I was at the back of the blockhouse, with my arms bound. I caught Jeff Mullins's eye. 'Jeff,' I whispered, when he came over—" and here she illustrated her pleading, melting expression—" 'Jeff,' I whispered, 'these bonds hurt me.' So he loosened them a little—and in a brace of shakes, when his back was again turned, I wriggled out of them and shot out through the back door."

"Bravo!" Dick applauded; and next he exclaimed, "Now for business." He told off two men to accompany him with a flag of truce, but, before going, he turned to me. "Ah, there you are, Ned!" he greeted me, quite brazenly. "Come now, you needn't frown so; you look better when you smile, my lad. Would you mind tellin' us how you hid out?"

Seeing no reason to remain silent, I cleared my dry throat and told him, briefly enough. He laughed pleasantly, like a man who has nearly lost a chess move to a friend.

"Only for Belle, here, you'd have given us the slip to-night. You see, men, what we owe her. Well, now, Ned, do you think that girl will come?"

I sensed so overwhelming a feeling of horror for his

duplicity and poise that my neck veins seemed about to burst.

"Cap'n Fogg is not the fool to let her come!" I cried in a voice as hoarse as a raven's. "You may do your worst with me, but he'll not let an innocent girl put her head in a lion's mouth."

"Put him under a tarpaulin," said Dick, not even losing his temper. He smiled. "We mustn't let Ned overheat hisself in this here hot sun, you know."

So I was removed away from the fire, and secured with ropes, while Dick and his two mates started off for the palisade with a flag of truce.

**FROM WHERE I** lay alone under my awning I could see them reach the palisade, and hail the blockhouse.

Cap'n Fogg hobbled out on his crutch, Abe Kemp and Tom Newgate marching beside him.

They were not far from the blockhouse when Gwendolyn ran out. I saw Cap'n Fogg waving her back angrily, but she tossed her head and came on. She had doubtless guessed the import of the parley; or at least she knew that it directly concerned me. She came stubbornly on to the paling.

The conference was brief. I could hear no words, but saw by Cap'n Fogg's angry gestures that he was refusing the terms. Tiger Dick said something further; again the captain shook his fist; and the three buccaneers wheeled and started back.

"Well, I reckon you'd better get to prayers," Hardy Flintlock called over to me.

Cap'n Fogg and his comrades watched till Dick was some distance off, and then started to retrace their steps to the blockhouse. Gwendolyn accompanied the men. Her face was bent down, and she held a kerchief to her eyes. Her very shoulders expressed the depths of despondency and grief.

But apparently this was being exaggerated for the benefit of the skipper. She lagged behind a step or two; I saw the captain pause and throw out an arm, whether to comfort her, or whether in sudden suspicion I could not tell; but she was too quick for him, and whipped away like a deer pursued by wolves. Down the slope she flew, and took the palisade at a bound. Without once heeding the cries of her friends behind her she ran straight to Tiger Dick.

It made me feel suddenly sick and old. Life is worthwhile only when it is valued. In the extremity of my despair I wished that they had killed me rather than let me live to witness this. For her wondrous sacrifice had placed her where she faced worse than death.

Bound as I was, I could only lie helplessly under the awning, where they had placed me, while Belle Saunders, with a smile, and the words, "See how the tables change!" fastened Gwendolyn's wrists behind her back, and led her under another awning, out of my sight.

TIGER DICK WAS writing a note.

"You take that," he said, handing it to Long Tom Bellew, "and hail that lubber Tyron. I reckon that'll fetch him."

"Aye, aye, sir!" said Long Tom, grinning.

He pointed down the bay, where the *Bonny Lee* lay in shallow water, embedded on the sandy spit, and bow on to shore. She had heeled to port, so that her starboard side was for the most part clear of the tranquil surface of the bay, and steaming with the evaporation of the water under the rays of the hot sun. There, just below her boot top, were to be seen the jagged holes made by the eighteen pounders.

Tyron's men had rowed out to her, and were busy as bees, rigging slings and prizing off shattered planks from the *Bonny Lee's* punctured hull. The tide had started on a long, slow ebb. As the *Bonny Lee* now lay, those holes would not be submerged even when the tide ran in; and anyway, long before that the Britishers would have slapped in spare planks, jammed in fresh oakum, and be ready to pump her out.

"Why, by Judas!" cried Long Tom. "The lubbers should have her righted and afloat afore midnight."

"Well, even if they ain't molested, what of it?" Tiger Dick came back at him, with a smile. "They can't no ways put to sea, past that lower fort, I reckon!"

"There ain't much gets by you, cap'n!" Long Tom said admiringly, as he and a messmate started off with a flag of truce.

A half hour dragged by before Long Tom returned. With him came Beau Tyron.

"Ah, there!" Dick greeted him jovially. "Welcome to our camp, sir. There you see her with your own eyes. Fit and sound—*he-he!*—as a spanking brig, just off the ways at Clyde. Maybe not so loving as you'd like to have her, sir; but you'll have time to tame her sound, I shouldn't wonder... Bring the little lady out, lads, where milord can see her better."

They brought her out, rebellious and untamed, her black eyes scorching this titled rake who had hounded her into prison and who was now ready to sell his soul to hold her against her bitter will.

Upon him her scorn had little apparent effect. His dark face was flushed rather with a sort of perverted intoxication, brought on by her nearness; his hands began to tremble a bit, and he breathed unevenly; and suddenly he attempted to step close and crush her in his arms.

"Nay, nay!" Dick interposed, pushing him back, while the buccaneers laughed. "You deliver your end—then I'll deliver mine."

"Devil take you!" blurted Tyron, flinging his laced hat upon the ground. "What," he hoarsely demanded, "do you want?"

"Ah," returned the pirate, "that's more like it. Well, first off, I'll tell you about where you are fixed, right now. You can get afloat—unless we want to risk losses layin' you aboard. You can't get out, though, that's sure as shootin'."

**"WHAT?" TYRON GASPED.** "You mean you've manned that lower fort?"

"Just that, milord," smiled Tiger Dick.

"But it's not in service!"

"Ah, but it is, though. Plenty o' powder and shot, stored there when we cruised in the old *Typhoon*. No, you can't get out."

"I can lay to, here, and keep *you* from getting out, by Pollux!" Tyron snapped.

"Can you? Can you, now? Well, suppose you gets afloat. First move you make to fight us, up goes this girl to the yardarm!"

Beau Tyron glowered.

"And," Dick pursued his advantage, "you won't have much luck pushing the fight against us, nohow. Them hands o' yours," he pointed out shrewdly, "ain't much heart to fight, they ain't—save in self-defense. What do they get out of it? They're outnumbered already, too. What they wants to do is cut and run, and let a frigate come here and nail us afore we can refit."

Tyron slowly picked up his hat.

"Well," he said, "state your plan."

"You'll be busy pumping out and shifting cargo, and what not, after them holes is patched. Come dark, you get all o' your hands below. You'll be on deck and give us a signal. Some of us will board by the spit and some by the jolly boat. In a brace of shakes—"

"You'll have them hatches under, and cut every throat."

"Ah? Not by a jugful. Gentlemen o' fortune ain't much for slushing decks nor rolling rope yarn for chafing gear, they ain't. We'll work them hands o' yours, we will, till we've loaded the blunt aboard and is safe at sea. Then we'll clap 'em somewheres ashore. And that goes for you and this girl, of course."

Tyron licked at his lips; glanced at Gwendolyn; and was lost.

"Done—and be damned to you!" he cried, thickly.

"That's fine!" Dick answered, heartily. "Now, all you got to tell them swabs is that I sent out a flag of truce to propose a kind of armistice till we get new masts in the old *Vulture,* here."

Then they moved away, out of my hearing, doubtless discussing further details of the wretched transaction; and presently Gwendolyn was led back to her awning, and Tyron walked away to the south.

Think as I would, I could see no way out of this ghastly situation; but thinking of it only made me more and more weary. Before long Nature had her way, and I was sound asleep.

# 21

## BUCCANEERS' CAPTIVES

**I WAS AWAKENED**, shortly after dark, by the rough hands of men who picked me up and carried me to an awning next to the one in which Gwendolyn lay bound.

"That 'll place 'em where you can keep your deadlights on 'em that much easier, Belle," said Tiger Dick. He and a large party of his buccaneers were preparing for their move upon the *Bonny Lee,* and calling Bruno and two others sharply by name, he added,

"Mind you, now! She's in command o' the guard here. I trust her. *She'll* not be tipping up a bottle when she should be lookin' sharp for signs of a rescue party. Mind you give her no trouble, either, or you'll have me to settle with!"

Shortly afterward, he and his men had melted into the tropical darkness, leaving Belle sitting on an up-ended cask near the fire, and two of the buccaneers talking in low tones just outside the yellow circle of light. Bruno I presumed to be doing sentry duty near the creek, against a sortie from our blockhouse.

The awning had been pitched on sticks, to form a three-walled tent. The front—facing toward the water and the fire—was open.

I lay on my right side, facing the fire; Belle was between

me and the blaze, and turned so that I could see only a part of her profile; but even though she only glanced round over her shoulder occasionally, I knew that the slightest movement on my part would bring her round about.

Some fifteen minutes went by in this manner. Now and again Belle glanced to south'ard, or cocked an ear in that direction; and I knew that my guards were waiting anxiously for sounds of conflict aboard the *Bonny Lee.*

No sound came from that direction… and then I sensed, rather than heard, that some one was behind me! Some one had crept in under the rear flap without so much as a single sound to betray his presence.

Next I felt a faint breath stirring the hair at the back of my neck, and knew that a sharp knife was passing noiselessly through the hempen strands about my wrists! Then utter amazement left me breathless: for there was Bruno, bending over me!

He frowned and shook his head slightly, cautioning me to silence. He was watching Belle intently, his horrid, bearded features contorted into a grimace of hate and jealousy.

What he was doing came home to me in a rush of delirious joy. He hoped to discredit the woman with his master, Tiger Dick, by conniving at our escape and then in some manner throwing the blame upon her.

I felt him pressing the flat of the blade against my wrist, which let me know that he was leaving the knife. With this I was to cut my bonds at the ankles, at the first opportunity. **SUDDENLY BELLE STIRRED** and started to turn her head. With the swiftness of a panther Bruno threw himself upon me. His hairy hands seized my throat; he flopped me over on my back, so that the knife was covered; and with the deep growls of a beast he pretended to crush my throat between his clutching fingers.

"Bruno!" roared Belle, whipping out a pistol. "Shiver my sides, but I'll drill you like so much pork if you don't let go."

The wily little ape-man arose with a great show of reluctance. He bared his yellow fangs at her, growling. As the other two buccaneers joined Belle, he stepped out into the firelight.

"So this is the way you do sentry-duty!" rasped Belle. She whirled the little man about and kicked him heartily. "Get to your post!" she thundered. "So help me Davy Jones, I've more than a notion to drill you through the back!"

When Bruno had disappeared in the dark, she shook her head and came into my tent. "Are you all right?" she asked, not unkindly.

I breathed deeply, and gasped, "Yes—after I get—some more air." If only she did not look at my lashings!

She made no effort to turn me over. Apparently satisfied that her hostage was unharmed, she went out again and sat down on her cask. "Did you ever see anything to beat that little ape?" she asked one of the buccaneers. "Why, I do believe he'd rather kill than roll in his coach, with a million safe in bank."

"He beats me, ma'am," growled the man. "I've seen some rough hands in my time, but that Bruno would make a man spew up hot scouse on a calm sea."

They laughed grimly at this, and then subsided into their former quiet.

What was I to do now? I dared not move. The two buccaneers did not move to their former positions, but remained near Belle. The three were now within a few feet of me.

Despite this I did not lose hope. Bruno was surely not so stupid as to leave matters as they were. So I lay quiet, counting off each leaden second.

It seemed an age before the pirates under Dick began yelling exultantly. They were aboard the *Bonny Lee*.

"They've taken her, they've taken her!" cried Belle, in keen delight.

At that there was a frightful commotion in the brush to north'ard. A pistol cracked, followed by another; and we heard Bruno squealing and gurgling excitedly, and charging toward the upper slopes, as though trying to capture an enemy who had been surprised while trying to creep up on the camp.

"Don't let the swab get away!" Belle cried out, running to aid him. The two buccaneers followed close in her wake.

"Bruno staged that whole show!" I thought exultantly. My hands were already free, and it was the work of a second to grab the knife and slash the ropes around my ankles. Into Gwendolyn's tent I bounded; in a jiffy she was free; and then I plunged with her into the dark ferns just behind the tents.

**TO RUN SILENTLY** through that tangle of vines and bushes in the darkness was impossible. No sooner did we strike the trees than our flight was discovered. The panting, swearing buccaneers fired in our direction as quick as winking, three pistol balls cutting branches close to us.

Seizing Gwendolyn's hand, I sped with her directly into the open and southward along the beach. There were no vines to trip us here. And how we ran! Shots followed us, but these were fired at two figures who were swallowed by the dark.

While Belle and her comrades chased us for some distance we drew farther and farther away till, arriving opposite a dune, we whipped round it and crouched. We were midway between the camp and the schooner.

Aboard the vessel several links had been lighted, and Tiger Dick was calling out across the water, with fierce oaths, wanting to know what the commotion portended. Behind us Belle had slowed to answer him; some of the buccaneers aboard ship were leaping down into a gig to come ashore; and it was obvious that we must act quickly, or be cut off.

"Can you swim?" I whispered.

"Like an eel," she answered.

"Then come," I urged.

I was already barefooted; she had but to slip off her low shoes; and we both were lightly clad. Clothed in a sailor's knee breeches, as she was, her limbs were as free as mine. We ran noiselessly down the sandy beach, waded hand in hand into the quiet water, sank in, and started swimming for the opposite shore.

This was nearly a mile away. It was so dark that I could barely make her out as she swam along by my side. They had not discovered this ruse, had the buccaneers, but were lighting torches and running here and there about the beach.

Soon their curses grew fainter, and still more faint; and by keeping the lights on the schooner nearly astern of us, and turning now and then to float upon our backs, we came at last to the other shore.

Wading in the shallow water toward the dry beach, I threw my arm around her waist, and drew her close. Tired as I was with the long swim, I nevertheless held her with a fierce grip, as though I would never allow her to go free again. It was difficult for me to realize that she was actually safe beside me.

"I'll never understand you!" were my first words when we halted on the beach. My arm was still around her. "You mocked me, and then risked your life, and more, to save me. Ah, if you loved me like that, why the devil—"

She interrupted me by drawing back from my eager lips. She drew a long breath; I thought—hoped—she was struggling within herself. Nevertheless she managed to push my arms away.

"Gracious, my hair must be a sight!" she exclaimed irrelevantly. Her hands fluttered to her damp tresses.

"A sight?" I expostulated, both hurt and amazed. My eyes, accustomed to the darkness, were entranced by the luxuriant cascades of black hair, tumbling down over her shoulders. I told her hotly that she could never be unsightly; that no woman had more lovely tresses, or sweeter mouth, or lashes half so beautiful. Then I rushed on: "But why, when you've shown you love me, do you hold me off?"

**HER BREAST ROSE** and fell, but she looked up quite demurely, while her fingers played with a lock which she had drawn over one shoulder.

"Love?" she said. "I did but pay a debt. La!" Thus she dismissed the whole subject of love, as though it were something to scorn. "I've worn the ball and chain *once,*" she reminded me. Then she looked down, and up again, and down once more, and finally up into my eyes as I stood glowering.

She threw back her head and laughed. How was I to guess that part of this was due to the hysteria of relief? She laughed uncontrollably, peal after peal.

I'll give you up!" I cried, with a weary gesture.

She straightened and sobered, or at least she ceased to laugh.

"That's better," she said. "Having quite made up your mind that I am hopeless, let's shake hands and be good friends."

I nearly refused her extended hand, but presently shrugged hopelessly and gave in.

"That's better still!" she declared, springing up. "And that reminds me, sir—how dare you keep the good ship's cook from her galley, sir? Cap'n Fogg will give us thunder if we don't round to and get back to duty."

I laughed at this and reluctantly arose. While we were free of the buccaneers, their capture of the *Bonny Lee* had placed our small party in a position wherein it was hard to see a ray of hope. Yet our fortunes were cast with that stout little band within the stockade, and we set out to rejoin them.

# 22

## THE PIRATE ATTACK

**WE RECEIVED A** vociferous welcome when we arrived. How they crowded round and clapped me on the back, and shook Gwendolyn's hand, and blessed and chided her for a madcap in a thousand, all in the same excited breath! As for Cap'n Fogg, he blew his nose violently, threatened to put Gwendolyn in irons if she disobeyed again, and pinched her ear by way of ferocious emphasis.

"A glass all round to celebrate this!" he cried. And when this was done he added: "There, now, that's enough of this folderol. Mr. Newgate, have you forgot your duty? Be off, sir, with your hands, to finish the work."

It was then that I first noticed several small, brass-bound chests in one corner, stained with dirt. In the top of each was burned the name:

*"Typhoon."*

"You're rifling the cache!" I cried excitedly.

"We are," said the skipper, as Tom Newgate and three of the men went out the rear door. "It's not so far up the slope to north'ard, and it appeared to be our best chance of rescuing you two."

"By offering to give up the money without a fight, sir?"

"Exactly. We took a vote on it, and every one said 'Aye.'"

I thanked him as a man in a million, but this sort of thing always flustered him. He waved it aside, quite brusquely.

"Now that you're back," said he, "we'll get the rest of it, and hold it for another purpose. They've got the ships, that's true. If we can beat them off—they won't be packing now, and leaving us to starve, by Judas. That money will hold 'em here like a kedge."

When I had eaten, I fell to with my watch, and helped to bring in the remainder of the chests. Jed Morgan and his messmates had buried the doubloons not more than four furlongs to north'ard of the blockhouse. There were forty chests, so small that a seaman could carry two, one under each arm.

From the sounds that came to us from the harbor, meantime, it appeared that all hands were having no little trouble in getting the *Bonny Lee* off the spit. So we were not molested, and before midnight had the last chest safe within the fort.

"There!" said the captain, when the chests were piled. "That'll bring 'em around our ears like a hornets' nest, I shouldn't wonder. However, we'll give them something of a surprise."

He pointed at the carronades. Formerly these small howitzers had pointed toward the bay through portholes, at the level of the floor, in the southern wall. They were still in this position, but three new ports had been cut in the blockhouse. Now the little guns could be quickly wheeled to any one of the four walls.

"It's not likely they'll board us directly in the face of those guns, but by one of the other sides," said the skipper. "Well, we'll be ready for them."

**NO ALARMS OCCURRED** throughout the rest of the night, and when I awoke, about daybreak, there was the *Bonny Lee* riding at anchor once more, not far off the stern of the beached *Vulture,* while the British sailors and soldiers, now the prisoners of the buccaneers, and shackled with the leg-irons so recently discarded by the convicts, were unloading stores from the dismasted hulk on the sands and transporting them, on one of our lighters, aboard the *Bonny Lee.*

To westward, keeping well out of gunshot of the block-house, a large party of the buccaneers were heading toward the plateau at the base of Tops'l Hill. They carried shovels with them.

"They'll find some monkeys playing around, maybe," said Abe Kemp, grinning. "But will you tell me what is that hanging from the crosstrees, cap'n?"

The skipper peered at the *Bonny Lee* through his long brass telescope. "Ah!" said he, with a deal of satisfaction. "They've given Bruno a hemp necktie and saved some hangman a job."

I took a look myself, and saw that this was true. The dwarf had reckoned without woman—and so, like many another man, had come to grief. I had him to thank for our release, but when I considered the motives that actuated him I could find no pity in my heart for the twisted form that dangled above the deck of our schooner.

We hurried through breakfast, and stood ready for a blow. At any minute now we might be boarded. The captain ordered the heavy door in the north side closed and barred, and called us to attention. He was a bit gray about the gills, with all the exertion and excitement, but stood stiff and upright upon his crutch, and grim and tight about the mouth.

"No use telling you," said he, "that this will be nip and tuck, and a close haul to a lee shore. Mercy we needn't expect. You're outnumbered three to one, but you're well able to see them all doing a right about, if you keep your heads. There's the chief rub. You have more to fear within yourselves than from them, my lads. Keep cool, and aim well, and we'll stand them on their ears. Get excited, and we're lost."

In the skipper's original scheme of defense a table was placed in the center of the rectangular room, laden with extra weapons. Near this he planned to stand, a cutlass on the table near him, and several pistols hanging ready to hand from a bandolier on his breast.

Abe Kemp and Tom Newgate were to man the carronades, while the rest of us were stationed as follows: Wheaton and Cairnes on the east, Digby on the west, Gwendolyn on the south, and Mullins, Traynor and myself at portholes in the north wall. The trees being closest to the paling on this side, it was from that quarter we might look for the worst part of the squall, the skipper reasoned.

"Stand ready, though," he said, "to shift sides as I may direct. On no pretext must any man leave his post without orders."

**WE WERE ALL** very serious and very attentive, and more than a little nervous. Yet there were no grumblers among us that morning; none of us had seen fit to question the captain's disposition of his forces. Each man had a loaded musket in his hands, while beside him, leaning against the wall, each musketeer had seven or eight extra pieces, all loaded and primed and ready to snatch up in turn. Our pistols we had thrust into our waistbands, and each man had a cutlass propped against the logs, close at hand.

For a time the morning coolness remained in the air, and the tree tops were vague and blurred in the soft mist that swam lazily upward from the moss beneath. This haze lay like a mantle over the southern end of the harbor.

Then the sun came into full view above the pines on Kidd's Neck; the rifts in the haze grew wider and wider till the craggy faces of the bare cliffs could be seen above the trees to north'ard; and presently the coolness gave way to a burning heat, which bathed the sands in a sheen of gold and set the resin to bubbling in the thick pine logs of the blockhouse.

Throughout this period we could catch no glimpse of the buccaneers. So as much as an hour and a half crept slowly by. We hardly spoke within the inclosure; we were damp with perspiration, and straining to catch the first signs of movement; and all of us were beginning to fidget and wish that they would come and have it over with, when there came a cry from Gwendolyn:

"They're loading the guns on the schooner!"

"I'd seen that," returned the skipper easily. "They'll amount to nothing more than noise, save for a chance hit directly through a porthole. Look sharp now! I expect they'll be boarding us right atop this bombardment."

"They're ready with the torches, sir!" said Gwendolyn.

The three starboard guns aboard the *Bonny Lee* shattered the stillness a second later, and the whole house trembled from stem to stern as the round shot plumped fair into the logs. I admit that I dodged sidewise a little, though I kept my eyes to the north.

"Stand fast all!" the skipper encouraged us. "See how those logs hold, with the dirt between."

This was indeed encouraging, yet there was still the fear that a round shot might crash through a southern porthole and wreck the place. The skipper read our thoughts, for within a minute, when the buccaneers aboard the schooner were once more ready with their torches, he warned us sharply.

"This will not last long. They'll start the attack right after one of these broadsides, and you may lay to it. Don't fire till you get the word."

Before the last word left his lips the cannon roared anew, and two round shot jarred the walls with terrific thumps. Not so the third. It screeched through one of the south ports and smashed, like a fiery comet, full into the logs between myself and Traynor. The jar filled the room with flying particles of dust.

I remember that moment as a sort of horrid blur, in which white faces stared oddly through the dust and were all well-nigh stampeded. Then the skipper roared:

"To your quarters! Here they come!"

# 23

## THE BATTLE AT THE STOCKADE

**NOT A BUCCANEER** could I see to north'ard, but the woods were ringing with loud huzzahs, and from the tail of my eye I saw a half dozen pirates dash out of the trees to eastward and run for the paling that surrounded the blockhouse.

"The carronade, sir?" cried Tom Newgate.

"No!" barked the skipper. "Cairnes and Wheaton, blaze away!"

The two men at the eastern portholes threw up their muskets and the room rocked with the thunder of the reports. Newgate and Abe Kemp were still being held in the center of the room with the two carronades, ready to wheel them wherever the skipper directed, and I was wondering why at least one of them was not pushed to the east wall, when from out of the forest to north'ard burst a dozen or more of the buccaneers, with Tiger Dick and Belle Saunders at their head.

Then I thanked the skipper for his coolness. The first six had hoped to startle us and throw us into confusion before the main body launched its assault!

"You may commence firing on the north," said the skipper, as cool as you please. "Carronades to north'ard!"

Tom and Abe Kemp thrust the first little howitzer through the new port in the north wall, and waited tensely, while Mullins, Traynor and I added to the din from the east wall with one rocketing report after another.

The buccaneers came up to the paling on the run, and started swarming over. We fired as fast as we could aim, and through the drifting smoke I saw two fall—one as he reached for the paling, and another just as he threw a leg over.

Then, seeing Tiger Dick forking a leg across the top, I took quick aim and pulled the trigger. I had the satisfaction of seeing him throw up his arms and tumble backward to the sand, the red blood spurting from a wound in the head.

But this in no wise checked the buccaneers. They were hell-bent to get that money and wipe us out. Long Tom Bellew and Hardy Flintlock roared like bulls; and their comrades, gripping cutlasses and pistols, vaulted over the fence behind them, and came racing up the slope toward us.

"Now!" roared the skipper, behind me.

Instantly Tom Newgate applied the torch, and the first carronade belched out a sheet of flame, scattering slugs with a thunderous report that seemed to lift the very roof.

That salvo came in the nick of time. The little carronade scattered her huge charge of musketballs like a bird gun.

A tornado of lead whistled and screeched all round the pirates' scarfbound heads.

The unexpected blast stopped them dead. One, I saw, was killed outright; two or three more dropped their cutlasses and clutched at streaming wounds; and two others left their weapons on the field and disappeared over the fence.

**BUT THIS TEMPORARY** check to the larger party on the north side did not spell victory for the defenders of the blockhouse by any means.

Of the six pirates who ran forward to scale the eastern paling, only one had been shot down outside the fence. Though Cairnes and Wheaton fired rapidly, five roaring cutthroats poured over the eastern uprights with their bright blades gripped between their yellow teeth.

One more fell to his hands and knees, inside the pickets—a London pickpocket who immediately scrambled to his feet, went back over the paling like an eel, and showed a clean pair of heels in reaching the shelter of the forest. But the remaining four were seamen who had sailed with Dick in the old *Typhoon*.

These leather-lunged villains came on with a rush, rallying their comrades to north'ard with blood-curdling yells; and though Cairnes and Wheaton fired frantically, those four raging scoundrels were abreast the eastern portholes in a twinkling.

Here was the very deuce to pay. These four were in position to sweep the room with pistol fire, while Long Tom Bellew and Hardy Flintlock were rallying their followers on the north. Those men were already halfway up the incline, and I saw that at least a half dozen of them were again starting forward.

In that second of time the battle hung in the balance. And everything happened with the rapidity of lightning.

The room was filled with an inferno of sound. Smoke filled the place; reverberating roars, the cracking of pistols, frightful groans, lurid oaths and wild incoherent cries contributed to the hideous din. Yet, for all that, some

*Dick forked a leg across the top of the stockade*

remained desperately cool, and were the means of staving off disaster.

A second after the four brutes fell so ferociously upon the defenders of the east wall, a pistol ball seared my forehead. I staggered back, blinded with blood. As I dashed it away I saw poor Cairnes whirl and fall heavily. There was a horrid blue hole in his forehead. The snarling ruffian who shot him loomed in the square port, but was himself shot down by Cap'n Fogg.

Another buccaneer fired two pistols point-blank at Wheaton. This quiet chap cried out in agony, and slumped down like a heavy sack.

In another heartbeat the remaining three demons would have been through the ports and upon us with their cutlasses. But the skipper was snatching out pistols and firing with both hands. Gwendolyn whirled from her port and charged across the room with a cutlass, her face as red as a sheet of flame in the swirling smoke. Her blade streaked downward through the air and clashed with a shower of sparks against the upraised cutlass of a tattooed rascal who had advanced far enough to throw one leg across the sill.

Her weapon was only partially deflected, and cut the fellow across the cheek. With a yell he fell back, and as flying splinters and whistling pistol balls drove the other two away from the portholes they had seized, the eastern wall was cleared.

"To the door, lads, the door!" roared Long Tom Bellew from without.

I LEAPED BACK to my porthole as they came on. All my muskets were empty, and I had only pistols left. Like Traynor and Mullins I fired repeatedly, but in the excitement and confusion must have taken poor aim; for the three buccaneers from the east side ran past me, and with Long Tom and a half dozen more to swell their numbers, fell like so many butting bulls upon the door in the north wall.

"In, in!" bellowed Long Tom, in a fever of rage and bloodlust.

*Crash!* came their heavy, muscular bodies against the door. They seemed to have the strength of giants. A panel split from top to bottom. The heavy oakdoor buckled and threatened to crack.

"At her again, all-l-l hands!" Long Tom roared.

They had apparently drawn back for another concerted lunge, and at least four of their comrades had rallied and were running back to come over the fence, when Abe Kemp jerked back the second carronade and trained it on the door. The four reserves reached the fence; the boarding party lunged at the door; the bar broke, and the door split asunder; and then Abe Kemp applied the torch.

There was a terrific explosion, and a heavy charge of slugs blew the door into kindling wood, and bowled over the buccaneers, helter-skelter, like so many ninepins.

"Board 'em, lads!" cried the skipper.

All who were able seized cutlasses and charged for the door. Out into the sunlight we poured, panting and eager, and fell with slashing saber blades upon the luckless gentlemen of fortune.

Had the charge from the carronade had a few feet more in which to spread, it is likely that most of the men before that shattered door would have been either dead or mortally wounded. As it was, two were dead, near the sill, and all but two had been wounded. Most of them had been knocked off their feet.

They came up in a bound as we fell upon them; but they were blinded with blood, and badly shaken; and in far less time than it takes to tell of the affray we knew that the tide was turning. Old Tom Newgate led us.

Long Tom Bellew saw him and raised his cutlass aloft with a roar of fury. Before it could be brought down, Newgate had slashed the ruffian's crimson face with a cut that brought his long form clattering to the ground.

Hardy Flintlock charged at me, but my cutlass met his at the guard and sent it whirling yards away across the bright sands. Weaponless now, he turned and ran for the fence, his blue face smeared with a patch of red. I was almost upon him; in fact, had raised my blade to cut him down when, in his eagerness to overtake another fleeing pirate, Mullins tripped me and we both plunged to the earth.

We were up like monkeys, but our chance was gone. Wounds or no, Hardy and his companions flew over the fence and away for safety. So did the four faint-hearted thieves who, but a moment before, had been about to recross the paling. Like deer they sprinted for cover. They paused not even to help Belle Saunders, who had picked up Tiger Dick bodily, and was carrying him into the woods.

Two more were still within the inclosure, but were running like antelope from the field.

One fellow, with a blue scarf, was pursued by Abe Kemp. Outdistanced, Abe whirled his cutlass about his head and threw it. The hilt struck the buccaneer in the nape of the neck. The fellow gasped; his arms flew wide; his head snapped back in an odd posture, between his shoulders; and down he fell, with a broken neck.

The last pirate was more lucky, for though Traynor, with his teeth showing in a ferocious snarl, was close upon him, the man vaulted and reached the top of the paling. Traynor's slashing cut missed the fellow's leg by an inch, and the blade wedged in a paling. Before Traynor could jerk the thing away the pirate had made his escape.

"Pistols, lads, pistols!" thundered the skipper, from the doorway.

But there were no more firearms loaded among us. In a moment the remnants of the attacking force was screened from view behind the ferns.

# 24

## LAST RESORT

**WE RETRACED OUR** steps toward the log house. The victory was ours. Of more than a score who had gathered to attack us we were certain that at least six were dead. One lay just outside the fence, while five lay sprawled in unnatural postures, within the inclosure, their glazed eyes staring at the pale blue sky.

Nor were these six dead men the only casualties suffered by the desperadoes. Tiger Dick and two others had been wounded in the act of scaling the paling. Of these, Dick had been carried away by Belle Saunders, a second had jumped up and legged it, while the third was still in sight, crawling painfully toward the brush.

Inside the inclosure two more lay groaning, at the point of death. One had been shot down by the skipper, and breathed painfully beneath one of the eastern portholes. The other lay near Tom Bellew's dead body. He had been riddled with slugs and cut down by Digby's cutlass.

This was a source of deep satisfaction; for, even as we hurried back to the log house, I reckoned up, and concluded that the buccaneers could not now muster more than a dozen who were free of wounds.

"The king-pin o' the lot may be headed for the long

shore, too!" panted Abe Kemp. "Ah, but the shot that laid him low was the luckiest o' the lot for us."

But when we poured into the fort, and the skipper brought us to heel after a brief period of excited clamor in which every one was talking at once, we sobered under the realization that our victory had not been purchased for a farthing.

Abe Kemp and old Tom Newgate—who were immediately placed on watch, and set to loading firearms—had been the only two to escape unhurt. Moreover, death had already claimed poor Cairnes and Wheaton.

In the matter of injuries, we found that a bullet had furrowed through the flesh under Gwendolyn's left armpit. Cap'n Fogg had been further wounded in the left shoulder blade by a splinter. Digby's left forearm was laid open from elbow to wrist by a saber stroke, and a pistol ball had plowed through the muscles of Mullins's right breast, passing out under the armpit. And Traynor was gashed in the thigh, while I had been nicked on the forehead by a pistol ball.

Having no medical supplies, we did what we could for the wounds, with cold water and hot tar, while those who were able, at the skipper's direction, joined in and put our stronghold to rights.

Throughout this period there were no further demonstrations of hostility on the part of the pirates. It wasn't long till we sighted them coming out of the woods to the south and west of us, and heading for their camp. At least three were being helped along, but we were sorely disappointed when we saw Tiger Dick walking, with a scarf bound round his head.

"The man has the lives of a cat, burn him!" grunted the skipper.

**FOR A TIME** we were not certain that Dick would not rally his surviving villains, and return to the attack. We could see him gesticulating and walking about like a caged lion. But his men lay back, or squatted under the awnings, in sullen attitudes; and presently Dick threw out his hands in a gesture of contempt and resignation. Soon afterward we saw that the prisoners were resuming the labor of removing supplies from the *Vulture*.

"We sunk the cream o' *that* lot!" said Abe Kemp, with a deal of satisfaction. "Since the beginning o' this show, there's been eight o' those *Typhoon* swabs gone to feed the sharks. They was the backbone o' the lot—and now, by gum, the rest that's left above-board has got a bellyful of fightin', I reckon."

While this relieved all of us, the excitement had died away, the reaction had set in, and I saw that Mullins and Digby were pale and drooping. Now that the first elation of victory had passed, and we saw that winning the fight had not materially bettered our situation, we were beginning to look down in the mouth.

What mattered it—so most of us were plainly thinking—if the buccaneers did not attack again? And what mattered it if we had the gold? We could not get away with it, having no ship. There it was: we had the gold and the stockade; they had the schooner, afloat, and the dismasted *Vulture* on the beach; and our gold would hold these pirates to the island like a kedge. They were in excellent position to sit tight and starve us out.

"What's the good of hanging back like two bulldogs at

either end of a rope?" Mullins finally spoke up. "Offer to
let 'em take the blunt and go hang!"

"Aye!" said Digby. "A lot of good it will do us, dead of
starvation."

Cap'n Fogg withered them with a wintry eye. "If I
thought they'd keep their word, I'd bargain for the *Vulture!*"
he cried. "But would they keep their word? No, by thunder!
They'd hang right here till we're starved out, and cut every
throat just as though we'd never came to terms."

All the rest of us promptly spoke up at this, to reassure
the captain of our support and full accordance with his
belief.

"Far better to die fighting than at the hands of torturers!"
Gwendolyn stoutly declared.

"Or by our own hands, at the last, if it comes to that,"
said Abe Kemp. "Give us your plan, cap'n, and we'll act
according."

"Thank you, my lads," said the skipper. To Mullins and
Digby he said: "Better get some sleep, my lads, and you'll
feel better." Then, after a stiff brandy all around, the skipper continued:

"My own plan right now is to sit tight and keep a sharp
watch, and beat them off if they come at us again. Mark
my words, they'll be discouraged in the long run. Then, if
they go packing, we'll put the old *Vulture* into commission.
Meanwhile, we must keep up our courage and whistle for
a wind."

It was my personal opinion that the skipper was nearer
despair than any of us—he carrying the responsibility of
leadership—and that he was merely talking through a
cocked hat, as the saying goes, to buck us up.

**IN THE MEANTIME** an idea had taken hold of me, and had pervaded my consciousness with stubborn tenacity throughout the day. As yet I had not spoken of it, for fear of being laughed at; but late in the afternoon something occurred which loosed my tongue.

This was the appearance of a cloud of smoke from the hull of the *Vulture*. The buccaneers had taken all they wanted from her and were destroying the beached ship by fire!

"There," said Gwendolyn, "goes our last chance for a ship!"

"Not by a jugful!" I cried hotly. "There's the schooner."

She grinned with irony and said dryly: "I only saw you take two drinks o' brandy."

"It isn't the brandy, and it isn't this scratch on the head either," I retorted. "Look!"

I pointed at the camp. Some of the buccaneers were shifting the tarpaulins nearer to the creek and away from the *Vulture's* smoking hull. This was of no particular import to us, but the prisoners were busy at quite another task. They were heaving and hauling with ropes and falls to move the black eighteen-pounders across the sands in the direction of the stockade.

"They'll make a breastworks of that sandy hummock, there," I declared. "And then what?"

She could but shake her head lugubriously. At the rate the heavy guns were being moved—and the task was a tedious one, the prisoners being forced to lay planking and sink "dead men" for their blocks and falls—the battery of four pieces would not be in position before night fell. By daylight, however, they would be ready to bombard our fort at a range of less than three hundred yards.

"Those walls won't stand up against *them* guns very long," Abe Kemp declared.

"Well, then," I cried, "we've got to make a try for that schooner."

My listeners smiled mirthlessly. But I had a plan ready. If, after dark, the others could get one of our carronades through a gap in the paling, sneak down the ravine with it, and give the buccaneers a surprise as they lay asleep, I'd have a try at boarding the schooner.

One good swimmer to go with me, I argued—Abe Kemp or Tom Newgate—and we had a chance, in the midst of the confusion, to knock out whatever sentries were aboard her, cut the cable, and run for it.

"The outgoing tide will favor us," I argued. "And look at those tree tops!" For a breeze was springing up.

**THEY STARED AT** me, aghast. Objections sprang to their lips. There might be sentries ashore, placed close to the palisade. We did not know how many men would be placed as watchmen aboard the *Bonny Lee.* My companion and I might be overpowered and captured.

"But even supposing you get the schooner—what then?" cried Mullins.

"You cut across the southeastern peninsula—Kidd's Neck, I mean—and wait till we sail down the bay, out the eastern channel, and pick you up. That's what."

The argument waxed hot and furious, with the skipper taking no part, at the last; only sitting back, his eyes on my hot face. Presently his lips began to quirk and his gray eyes sparkled.

"By gum!" he cried at last. "It makes me young again." And despite his lacerated leg he stood up and took two or three excited steps on his ungainly crutch. He clapped Tom Newgate resoundingly on his broad, muscular back.

"See there?" he exclaimed. He pointed: only two men were visible on the *Bonny Lee*. They were leaning over the bulwarks, talking to Tiger Dick and four others, who were about to shove off in a gig and return to shore.

"I think Ned's right!" the skipper declared. "I mean, I think we've got a chance. By hickory, we'll try it, and be damned to 'em!"

The fierce spirit of the crippled old gladiator quite won the day and swept the last of the lugubrious off their feet. Caught up by the infection, we flung our hats aloft and made the blockhouse ring with a loud sea cheer.

# 25

## NIGHT SORTIE

**DARKNESS FOLLOWED CLOSE** upon the heels of a blazing tropical sunset, a soft, dusky mantle blotting out the trees at the southern end of the harbor and dimming the outlines of the anchored schooner, with the black flag flying over her stern.

Soon her bare poles and furled sails were melting away into the ebony pall; soon we could not discern a line of her trig hull, her position being marked for us only by the yellow glow of light in her cabin ports; and before long the whole island was blanketed under an impenetrable shroud save for that spot at the northwest corner of the harbor where flames were still consuming the old convict ship.

In the immediate vicinity of that spot the scene was as light as day. Fanned by a steady offshore breeze, the crackling tongues of upshooting fire brought out the near-by palms in startling clarity. The flickering rays of light likewise played fitfully over the beached gigs, and the white tarpaulins pitched near the creek mouth, under which the swarthy, half-naked pirates were carousing.

Some of them, however, had an eye to duty, for we could see them driving their prisoners, with a rope's end, to haul three more guns toward the hummock. At first we feared that the drunken rascals might commence a bombardment as soon as the cannon were in place. But when the last of the eighteen-pounders had been pulled out of the circle of light, the hummock remained shrouded in darkness.

We breathed deeply in relief; the desperadoes had sensibly concluded that they needed daylight for the accurate gunnery which plants one shot atop another and so breaks through such thick walls as they must contend with.

When at last we were certain that most of the pirates and prisoners had returned to their fire, and we were ready to place our carronade in position, Abe Kemp made a suggestion.

"In two hours or so those swabs at the fire should be piped down," said he. "Anyways, you'll have plenty time to swim out to the schooner. Then, instead o' firing on those lubbers, I'll sing out that the party has left the blockhouse. Cap'n Fogg can throw in a few shots to make it better, see?"

"Which 'll bring those devils running for that gold as sweet as never was!" cried Tom Newgate, admiringly.

"Also, in case of need, like a rumpus aboard the schooner—for you may have some bad luck—I'll be ready to hand them suthin' as a remembrance, time they go racin' back to put off after you in the gigs," Abe added.

Reconnoitering, we made sure that no sentries lurked within the near-by trees. Then Tom, Abe and I grabbed up one of the small carronades, returned to the paling, and worried loose two of the uprights. In twenty minutes the little howitzer was in position at the edge of the trees which grew thickly between the western side of the clearing and the ravine.

Looking southward, nothing intervened between Abe

and the beach but a cleared slope; the pirates' big guns had been dragged into position a hundred yards or more to his left, and there he was, under cover, ready to sweep the slope with his scattering slugs if the pirates streamed across the space lighted by the burning ship.

"Why," said Abe, chuckling, "I've got a better seat than a box in a theayter, up here on this knoll."

So we left him, looking down on the pirates' camp, with a glowing rope's end ready to serve as his torch.

**WORKING ROUND PAST** the north side of the fort, Tom and I entered the woods and eventually reached the beach, far to eastward of the singing buccaneers. At no time had the light from the blazing hull extended to the anchored schooner, and we noted with satisfaction that the flames were somewhat lower. The British prisoners, we saw, were lying in a huddle at the south end of the camp.

Our next concern was the acquisition of a suitable drift log. After some search we came upon one, and, with a handshake for good luck, we tightened our belts, kicked off our shoes, and waded with it into the water.

We had brought with us no pistols nor anything else in the nature of a weapon, save our dirks. We made easy progress through the rippling water. Tom hugged the log at one end, and I at the other, both paddling with our free hands. We paddled straightway for the stern of the schooner, making no noise, and hoping that even if we were discovered, the watchman aboard would look upon the log as nothing but a piece of drift.

Nearing the ship, we could make out no sign of a sentry on deck. Nothing stirred above decks save the rigging, through which the offshore breeze played musically. Sailors call this the "topmast chantey." To this were added the other murmurs which always are heard about a ship at anchor—the lap of the ripples against the hull, the occasional thrum of the hawser, or the creaking of a swaying block aloft.

But in the cabin at the stern we heard voices. There the swinging light was burning brightly and the yellow rays streaming out of the stern windows to play upon the surface of the black waters.

To venture directly into that circle of light was out of the question. On the other hand, it was equally foolhardy to leap to conclusions: voices in the cabin did not necessarily prove that no other pirates lolled on the darkened deck.

So, instead of wearing down alongside, we worked round to her starboard counter, keeping out of the light, and came under her sloping stern.

Thus far we had been able to catch no distinguishable word from the cabin, nor could we recognize any of the speakers. Nothing reached us except a murmur, or the tinkling of glass, or the scrape of a cabin chair. Some of the pirates were seated about the cabin table, but who they were or how many we could in nowise determine.

This was baffling. By the sounds I guessed that not more than three were at the table; but guesswork was of little help here.

I was almost on the point of pushing for the bows, whether or no, when a commotion turned my attention shoreward.

Hardy Flintlock and four of his messmates were coming down to the beach, obviously to board a gig. In a moment it became plain that they were about to row round the stern.

We had no recourse but to sink heads under and hold our breath.

**ONE MINUTE IS** a long, long time to go without breathing. I think that I stretched the time, on this occasion to more than a minute and a half. My lungs were bursting when I at last surrendered and thrust my nose above the surface.

How I struggled to remain quiet, as my lungs sobbed for that reviving draft of air! For there were the five buccaneers, just swinging round the *Bonny Lee's* counter.

I sank again, my hand on the log. This time I remained submerged only a few seconds. When I came out again the men in the gig were nearing the gangway.

The tramp of their feet on the deck was the signal for me to grip Tom's hand.

"Tom," I whispered, as the buccaneers came tramping aft to the cabin, "let's chance it, forward."

"Aye," Tom returned. "We're doing no good here."

Accordingly, we pushed out with the log and paddled forward along the port side.

We were gambling on this assumption: if the reckless mutineers kept so poor a watch ashore, they would not, in all consistency, be better sentries afloat. They had—or so we prayed—all gone to the cabin, leaving no one on deck.

A few strokes, and the shadowy outlines of two gigs were discernible. They swung idly at the foot of the gangway.

"Here," I whispered to Tom, "is my chance. I'll lay aloft, and see what's topside."

In two shakes I was out of the water, and skimming up the gangway. Cautiously I poked my head above the top step. No one was in sight. Growing bolder, I raised up and scanned the deck. Not a trace of any sentry could I make out in that dark waist.

Quickly I slipped below, and told Tom. He was close upon my heels when I stepped again on the familiar deck of the *Bonny Lee*.

"The fo'c's'le, lad!" whispered the former buccaneer, seizing my arm and urging me forward.

Upon the planks our bare feet made no sound. He stole forward, encountering not a soul while *en route*, and popped into the fo'c's'le companionway.

Here we drew breath, listening intently for movements on deck. We could hear nothing beyond the usual murmuring of a wooden ship, nor could we see anything resembling a human form in the black shadows that enshrouded the waist.

The waiting and inaction irked me. All hands aboard ship being—so I believed—within the after cabin, I decided to lay aft and eavesdrop.

"Better not try for too much and lose all," Tom warned.

Against this I argued our ignorance of the pirates' plans, the silence on deck, and the possibility of learning something to our advantage. Reluctantly he gave in, and I stole aft.

I kept close within the shadows of the bulwarks as I went, but my caution was unnecessary. I might easily have walked the length of the deck without hindrance or discovery, for all hands, even as I had hoped, were gathered round the table in the skipper's cabin.

Abaft the mizzen were three steps, leading up on the poop deck. The middle of this deck was broken by the low cabin roof, in the sides of which were skylights. These

were open, for ventilation. Inasmuch as the companionway opened aft, I was enabled to crawl up alongside these
ports to peer and listen.

**THERE BELOW ME** were Tiger Dick, Belle Saunders, and
Beau Tyron, seated on the after side of the broad table,
facing forward; while on the other side were Hardy Flintlock and the messmates who had just come aboard with
him in the gig. These last appeared truculent and sullen,
and Dick's face was flushed and shining with the heat of
anger.

"Well, now," he said, shoving back a glass, "we've had
a drink all round, as the custom is afore the cap'n hears a
delegation, and I'm all ears to hear what it is you have to
say. You, Hardy," he added with a faint sneer, "are spokes-
men, so I take it. Well, then, speak up."

Hardy's blue face twitched nervously, and he cleared
his throat.

"We took a vote and you're to step down," he growled
bluntly.

" 'Step down,' eh?" Dick said softly. "Well, well! And
who's to take my place? You, Hardy? Ah, but you're coming
up the ladder hand over hand, Hardy."

Hardy licked at his lips, and gulped. But for the presence of his comrades I think the man would far rather have
faced a caged lion than the smiling, sneering, red-faced
giant whose black eyes mocked him across that oaken table.
But he summoned his courage, to keep his face before his
followers, and growled:

"This ain't no joke, Dick Buntline, as you'll find out.
We're within the articles, we are. *We're* ready to vote, too.
Suppose you lay ashore with us, and help us ballot."

Dick snorted. "And who's to make me?" He laughed unpleasantly. "Any one of you? Speak up, my hearties—any one or all." Suddenly he leaned forward, baring his white teeth. "Speak up!" he roared, with a vehemence that shook the cabin. "What son of a dog-eating rum guzzler here has the nerve to cock his hat at me? Shiver my sides, but let him speak! That's what I say—and I'll have his heart out on this table in a brace of shakes!"

The utter ferocity of the giant quelled his mutineers as landsmen quail before a blow. Not a man spoke. He eyed their pale faces a moment, and then sat back, and lit a pipe. Belle Saunders smiled.

"There's the answer to *that!*" said Dick, at last, blowing out a cloud of smoke. "Well, then, you say you're within the articles—which I'll grant." But he followed this with a slap on the table that made it dance. "Don't you forget this, though," he added. "You can't make me step down till I've heard what's eatin' the lot of you. Pipe up—and then we'll talk."

"Why, we're all to one way of thinking," stammered Hardy. "First off, you wouldn't let us go and dig up that gold. Consequence is, Tom Newgate led them swabs to it. Next thing: we don't aim to be hazed, bein' gentlemen o' fortune, and free. Nor that ain't all—the worst of it is this woman."

"So? What about her?"

"Hadn't been for her, we'd've had them two prisoners—that Ned Allen and that girl. You'll not be so brash as to deny that, by thunder!"

"Eh? Well, what would you have done with those prisoners if they hadn't got away?"

"Why, them swabs in the log house would have given up that blunt long since rather than see them tortured— that's what we'd have done with them. What's more, there wouldn't have been no attack, and so many brisk lads gone to feed the sharks."

"And I'd have had what I came across the ocean for!" cried Beau Tyron, with a bitter oath.

"Ah?" said Dick. "Maybe you're for standing in with Hardy, my lad." And when Tyron, who looked haggard, embittered, and utterly sick of his treacherous bargain, turned moodily and dejectedly toward a stern window, Dick resumed: "Well, Hardy, is that the full extent of your bilge?"

"It is, and we don't aim to have no more of it."

**"WELL, WE'LL SEE** as to that," said Dick. "Now, you say I wouldn't let you dig up that gold. Shiver my timbers, but is that a head or a turnip you have atop them shoulders, Hardy Flintlock? At the time you wanted to dig up that blunt this man Tyron was about to lay us aboard. By the ship's cat, but of all the leather-headed arguments put up by a lot o' lubbers, that's the cream o' the lot! If we'd set out for that blunt, we wouldn't have had no ship, nor no stores, nor nothing but *that* blunt."

"A few of us could have gone," growled Hardy.

"Yes? You know, if you know anything, that you wouldn't have trusted a few no more than you'd trust a bumboat man."

"That's right enow," conceded the seaman with the black sash. "Talk sense to 'em, cap'n."

"Sense, to them swabs, Bill?" cried Dick. His throat cords tightened, and he shook his pipe by way of red-faced emphasis to his vibrant, vehement outburst. "By thunder," he broke out, "but it's enough to turn a sensible man's stomach, dealing with the likes of them! All the makin's of a lot o' first class monkeys wasted in human forms. Why, by the gods, they're setting out to put me down when they can only hand and steer, and couldn't set a course if 'twere marked with red buoys. As for this woman—ain't nary a jackass in the mullet-headed lot got brains enough atween his ears to know that Ned Allen would have hidden safe aboard the *Vulture* till dark and then gone scot-free if it hadn't been for her! Then how would we have got that girl, and later, this schooner?"

His volubility as much as his logic frustrated and confounded the sullen mutineers. Before they could summon further words, Tiger Dick breathed deeply, and continued:

"I'll tell you what's wrong with most of you. You're out-and-out cowards—that's what. If I'd had my way we'd have attacked again, while they was shaken—and we'd have been counting gold right now, by thunder. But you'd had one good licking; I weren't there to finish the job for you; and now you've laid down on me, and aim to take the safe way, behind them guns.

"Gentlemen o' fortune? I reckon you'd look good in the saddles o' the horse marines! You won't fight; you can't keep more than one fact at a time afore your glimmers; and you can't sail the ship. Yet here you are, you lubbers, having the garfish gall to go and set a wooden head with a blue mug up as capting over *me!*"

He sat back, and eyed them witheringly, till they shifted

uncomfortably, finding no word at first to say. Then Hardy brought up one last point. Said he:

"You don't care how many of *us* is shot down getting that blunt, Dick Buntline. You—"

"Silence!" roared Dick. And when Hardy knuckled down, Dick said to Bill: "Lead these lambs ashore, Bill. Tell the rest of them gentlemen o'fortune that I'm waiting, calm but joyful, for to hear the results of the *next* election."

Seeing that the delegation was about to depart, I stole forward, and was once more alongside Tom when the first buccaneer came out of the after cabin, followed by Beau Tyron.

The rascals stopped and growled in talk, abaft the gang-way. Then all but two tumbled down into a gig, and pulled ashore, leaving the sullen pair smoking alongside the port bulwarks. Dick and Belle Saunders remained in the cabin. **AS MUCH AS** an hour or more dragged by, with no change in this situation, till Hardy Flintlock and three others again came down to the beach to board the gig.

They were soon aboard ship, and trooping into the after cabin. With them went the two who had remained on deck; and they had barely left the deck when a volley of musket shots resounded in the woods to north'ard of the blockhouse. Close upon this there followed a hail from Abe Kemp.

"So ho, mates! Ahoy, shipmates! Bundle out and bear a hand—the lubbers has deserted ship."

Clamor broke out ashore and afloat. The buccaneers at the camp fire leaped up and started racing for the palisade, while out of the after cabin burst a panting, eager squad. Over the side they went, and into a gig, afire with haste.

"They've left the gold, they've left the gold!" wheezed Hardy Flintlock, in a transport of joy. "Oars, mates, oars!"

"Avast!" cried Dick. "Here's all of us, deserting ship. Two of you back on deck, and lively."

There was a brief argument, a blow, and two disgruntled, cursing seamen came back on deck. The gig pulled shoreward, all hands crying out like children and pulling with might and main.

"It's here, mates, it's here!" bellowed a pirate's voice a moment later. It came from the direction of the log house—and from the throats of all the other buccaneers there broke a cry that was like nothing so much as the baying of wolves. One and all raced madly across the sands.

# 26

## BLIND STEERING

**THE TIME HAD** now come when Tom and I must act, but at Tom's whispered insistence we delayed until we were certain that the majority of the buccaneers ashore had entered the blockhouse.

There was also another consideration which stayed us. The two men left aboard the *Bonny Lee* remained for a time in the waist. We thought it best to delay a few minutes, in the hope that they would separate, or change their position.

The two were grumbling and growling like leashed dogs. At first we could not catch the words distinctly, and supposed they were cursing Dick for ordering them to remain aboard ship; but at last an angry outburst of oaths revealed the truth.

"Why, by the powers," cried one—and we recognized the voice of Bill, the fellow with the black sash—"you simply got to have discipline! Dick was right; it weren't good sense to burn that ship, nohow, till we had the blunt safe aboard."

"Hell—and haven't we got it now? It's as good as aboard, ain't it? Hardy had the right idea, with them guns."

To this the older buccaneer made a sulphurous reply, and I thought the two would come to blows on the spot.

But their voices subsided; and next we heard the splash of a bottle, and the two lurched aft.

"Now," said Tom, "we've got 'em bottled. They're after more rum."

Hardly daring to breathe, we started aft. We had picked up two belaying pins, and with these and our dirks in hand we tiptoed across the planks to the cabin skylights.

Before we reached them we heard a volley of oaths break out in the cabin. A chair overturned with a crash, and as I reached the first skylight, I peered within and saw Bill and his adversary, locked in each other's arms, struggling like two maniacs.

Here, there, and back again they swayed and lunged, tumbling chairs, upsetting the table, wrecking a cabin already littered with bottles and other traces of debauchery. Their eyes blazed murderously; their faces were black with the rush of thick blood; they wheezed and panted like embattled bulldogs.

"To the companionway!" I whispered, eagerly.

Old Tom followed me, but gripped my arm. "Wait!" he said. "One will fall in a minute."

His prediction was correct. There came a crash in the cabin, and we peered down the companionway. There, under the swinging light, Bill had pinioned his writhing antagonist upon the floor.

With a leap Tom sprang down into the interior. Bill had only time to throw up his head before Tom's belaying pin crashed down on his skull. He fell with a plop, like a spraddled frog, atop his half-choked victim. I was close behind Tom. It was the work of but a minute or so to secure the drunkards' pistols, truss them up, and gag them.

**AS SOON AS** that job was finished we ran on deck.

"We'll get the fores'l on her first, lad," panted Tom.

Never were furls cast loose or halyards jerked from cleats in faster time, I'll warrant. And how we heaved! Not with a song, 'tis true; but no seamen ever heaved with a better will.

Heave as we would, though, the fores'l was barely up and fluttering in the breeze, when there came a shout on shore. One of the buccaneers had been left on guard over the prisoners, it appeared.

"Ahoy, the ship!" he called. "Where bound, mates?"

We made no answer, being busy with sheets and halyards. And the suspicious fellow ashore turned and shouted to his fellows in the distant blockhouse.

"Shall I cut the hawser?" I asked Tom.

"Cut away," said Tom. "Lively now. We'll get a jib on her afterward."

I raced forward and slashed at the bucking hawser. Behind me the fores'l was slatting, and the schooner tugged at the hawser like a fretful horse at a hitching strap. Meanwhile the shouts of the buccaneers were ringing back and forth across the island, and they came thundering beachward, bound for the gig and jolly boat.

I lost my head, and hacked insanely, cursing in my impatience. Guessing trouble, Tom ran forward and told me to lay aft to the helm.

"You must only cut when she slacks," he said quite coolly.

Back I flew to the wheel. As I grabbed the spokes, the foremost pirates came raging into the light cast along shore by the blazing *Vulture*. At that moment Abe Kemp's carronade spoke from the plateau. A thunderous report rocked the island, and a fan-shaped sheet of crimson stabbed the black shadows. A myriad leaden pellets filled the air about the ears of the pirates and fell like hailstones into the bay.

This served to scatter the buccaneers; and before Dick could rally them, Tom severed the last strand and ran aft to pay off the sheet.

Before he reached it I had thrown over the wheel. Like a toe dancer taking the first mincing steps, the graceful schooner bobbed upon the rippling surface of the bay, till the boom swung outboard, the sail bellied taut to leeward with a sharp crack, the prancing bow came round, and we were gliding away to south'ard, with one of the gigs still trailing alongside.

We had started with not a second to spare, for with Dick roaring orders at them, a cursing, panting horde of buccaneers recovered from their confusion and tumbled into the other gig and jolly boat.

"Luff!" Tom called; and I brought her up to ease her till he raised the jib.

This maneuver lost nearly all the way we had, while behind us the buccaneers were laying to their oars like men making a race for life. Aided by the tide, they were rapidly overhauling us, when Tom cried: "Stand away!"

The slatting jib bellied out with a report like a gunshot.

I yelled excitedly, as the ship heeled slightly and paid away.

Tom came back on the double to peer anxiously astern. The buccaneers were clear of the light from the burning *Vulture*, but we could hear them plainly.

Dick was driving the crew in the gig like a Roman galley master, and we knew that his craft was fairly leaping out of the water with each stroke of her oars.

"They'll overhaul us, at this rate!" cried Tom. "We must bend on the mains'l, my lad."

This was ticklish work. We were sailing by instinct, so to speak; we could see neither shore abeam, nor anything at all save an ebony shroud, dead ahead; and it behooved us to keep well clear of outjutting spits, lest we run aground. Yet more sail she needed, and more sail we must get upon her. **TOM LASHED THE** wheel, and we piled forward, hearts in our throats. But we raised the mains'l without a hitch; and what a relief it was to see that boom swing outboard and to hear the canvas slat and fill! Ever gaining headway, it became apparent within fifteen seconds that we were drawing away from the pursuing boats.

Back at the wheel, old Tom gripped the spokes and peered sharply ahead.

"Thank our lucky stars that she's so sweet a sailer! But maybe we've cheered too soon, my lad. I can't nohow see for to set a course, 'cept by guess and by God."

"And what'll we do with those prisoners?" I asked.

"Ah!" said he. "That's right. Overboard with 'em, is my vote."

I jumped into the cabin and brought the two pirates to their feet. Bill was just recovering from the daze of the blow on the head. One at a time I bundled them to the rail, slashed their bonds and forced them to leap. The darkness in our wake swallowed them, though now and again we heard them cursing and hallooing to their comrades in the gig.

The sounds of the rowing behind us grew fainter, and still more faint, and finally ceased. We were by this time a quarter of the way toward the narrow passage which twisted to the south and west, between heavily wooded banks, and through which we must pass before reaching the outer or lower harbor and the adjacent, open sea.

We had now left the pirates behind, but were by no means out of danger. The stars were lighting the heavens, but all round the horizon lay a broad black belt. Against this background the tree tops were lost to view, appearing only as the lower part of an unbroken dark swath. We were not certain that we could pick them out until it would be too late to turn and avoid the shallows.

As for seeing the outlet, this was equally impossible until we came within a few ship lengths. Even in daylight a man in the interior of the upper harbor could not look directly out upon the lower harbor and the sea; for the passage, bending to the south and west, was lost between the trees.

"We must run for it, as best we can," said Tom. "One thing's certain, anyway—there's a strong scour with the ebb along this south shore, and though I can't see so well, I can hear the rips at the neck of the channel."

So we stood away, praying for luck, and peering with all eyes into the blackness ahead.

**FORTUNE FAVORED US** at the lower end of the harbor. We could discern the trees—very faintly, to be sure, but clearly enough to be certain.

Immediately old Tom brought her round to port. We knew that the entrance was to our left; for at last we could hear the splash and ripple of the rips.

"Cross your fingers, lad!" cried Tom. "I must stay this close in, to keep our bearings."

It was a swift run from here to the outlet, where the ebb ran like a millrace. Almost before we realized it, we were gripped by it, the bow whipped round to starboard, and away we went down the passage, the ship dancing like a cork on the churning surface and the foam boiling away from her sharp bows.

That was a moment in a lifetime! No sweeter music ever came to my ears than that made by our bows. I danced, I sang, I wept with the wild joy of it. Little had I realized the tension I had been under till this hope of freedom loomed so close. Now it seemed that every nerve within me had been released from a hideous bondage, and in my transports I shouted like any madman.

It was then that the blow fell. There were the black blurs on either side of that narrow channel, racing by us; a little lightening in the pall ahead showed us our first glimpse of the lower harbor; and then—*crash!*—the ship struck.

So heavy was the jar that I thought the sticks would be snapped out of her. Tom and I were knocked off our feet. Something cracked at the same time, aloft, and I heard a splash alongside. The sudden stoppage of the ship had snapped the rope which held up the forgotten body of the dwarf, Bruno, and flung it into the current.

I made no move to arise. Every bit of strength had deserted me. I just lay there, too sick at heart to move. We were hard and fast aground... and there, just showing the tip of her rim above the trees on the slopes below Tops'l Hill, was the damnable, tardy moon. The mocking, smiling, silvery moon that might have been the saving of us had we been allowed to wait a little longer before our ill-fated flight from Tiger Dick!

# 27

## ON A LEE SHORE

**OLD TOM'S DESPAIR** was even worse than mine. He sagged in the scuppers, weeping like an old, broken-down human derelict.

"Why," he sobbed out, "I thought I was doin' best when I volunteers to come, knowin' this harbor as I do—and me these many years at sea. But it's Fate, I tell you—it's downright Fate, and you can't beat that Tiger Dick. He's the son o' the devil hisself, I tell you."

Seeing him so crushed I suppose, was what roused me. I came slowly to my feet, went down into the cabin, found a bottle, and came on deck. I gave him a drink, took one myself, and told him not to take blame for the mishap. How the devil could mortal man steer into a black hat, so to speak?

"What's more," I cried—though I was hollow, and only talking to hear myself speak, as you might say—"what's more, we didn't ground at full tide, remember. And here's another point: Dick and his men can't see us. We're well sheltered behind the trees, even after the moon's up."

Old Tom stared at me, rubbed his face in his sleeve, and arose. "I'm a doddering old fool," he growled, with some of his old spirit. "Never say die! That's the talk. We'll look around."

The growing light of the rising moon soon dispelled the shadows in the passageway, and we saw that we were aground not far from the east shore. Hasty soundings proved that only the bows were hard and fast on the sand spit. Even at this low tide there still remained a fathom of water under two-thirds of her keel.

We talked this over. Provided that the demons did not come into the passageway beforehand, we might be able to work the *Bonny Lee* off when the tide turned.

"It wouldn't be any trick for a crew," said old Tom. "Take a line ashore, aft, to them trees." He pointed astern to a bend in the channel, not more than two ship lengths away. "Take a hitch around the capstan, and after the tide turns, take a pull at her, and off she'd slide, as easy as A B C. That is, if we had a crew."

There was the deuce of the situation. Tom and I could not hope to work her off unaided, and it was obvious that we must get in touch with our friends.

"They'll have to chance it, wounds or no," said Tom. "We risked everything on this—giving up the blunt and our stores and everything. If them swabs up there take it into their heads to row around, or come down the beach, they may catch us just about the time we get our party back here. It's life and death, and a close shave to a lee shore, I'm telling you. Only, if we don't risk it, we're as good as shark bait, and you may lay to it."

"They've got to risk it," said I.

So it was decided, and we next discussed the best means of bringing the others down to the stranded schooner.

**KIDD'S NECK, THE** peninsula which formed the eastern and southeastern side of Hangman's Bay, was not more than a quarter of a mile wide at any point. We had planned that after their demonstration with the carronade, the captain's party would make for the island's eastern coast.

They were to have taken the direct route, straight east from the blockhouse. They had not more than three quarters of a mile to travel, and though the night had been pitch dark till now, and they could not be expected, wounded as several of them were, to make rapid progress through the ravines and undergrowth, it seemed certain that they would have reached their destination by this time.

To get in touch with them it was of course possible for one of us to cross Kidd's Neck at once, and walk northward along the outer beach. But coming back, there would be the captain, hobbling on his crutch, and Traynor handicapped by a cut in the thigh. They would be able to cover the three miles at little better than a snail's pace.

"It'll be a hard pull for two, but there's the gig at the gangway," said Tom. "That's our best hold."

I agreed with this, and we set to work. If worse came to worst, and we rowed back only to find the buccaneers had discovered the schooner, we must be prepared as best we could to risk our lives at sea in an open boat. With this grim possibility in mind, we rolled out a water cask, some arms and powder, and such supplies as we could conveniently store, and took to the oars.

Though we had fairly easy rowing with the ebb into the lower harbor, past the fort and eastward between Camano and Capstan Sprit, we were in for a long, hard pull when we came outside, rounding the southeastern end of Camano

*They were in for a long, hard pull outside*

Island. For the breeze had veered, and the surf was rolling, the great combers sweeping down from the northeast and breaking in churning foam upon the sandy ocean beach.

What a row that was! I began to grow arm-weary before we had covered half the distance up the island to the point opposite the head of Hangman's Bay. I steadily became more and more apprehensive of making a safe landing.

"We'll swamp in this surf," I said to Tom.

"We'll drop the hook and swim ashore," said Tom. "Time the tide turns, you'll find this rip will ease down, too."

This heartened me, and I pulled with renewed energy; but it was past three o'clock when we neared our destination.

Overhead the moon was making of the heavens a wondrous dome flooded with mellow silver light. But, peer as we would, we could see no signs of our friends.

"This here's the place," said Tom. "I ain't lost my bearings."

"They *must* have left the fort!" I declared in perplexity.

"Well," said Tom, "we'll drop the hook here and see what's what."

We shot the anchor overboard, a hundred yards or more offshore, and plunged into the rollers.

**TIRED AS WE** were, that swim ashore was a stern adventure in itself. Where the gig rose and fell, at anchor, the moonlit rollers foamed at the top with a hissing, swirling rush of sparkling froth; and while the waves threw us shoreward, and there was no current to breast, this spray and rushing foam whipped forward from the curling crests and shot down into the hollows at express speed.

Over our heads it broke, swirling, lashing, suffocating—a whirling mist of suds, too light to lift us, yet thick enough to keep us gasping for air.

This was bad enough; but the closer we came to shore the briefer became the interval between the waves. They pounded us downward, buried us under tons of water, seemed to clutch at us with a thousand powerful, mocking hands which were determined to drag us back into the depths of the pitiless sea.

Four times I fought the undertow for a footing near shore, and four times lost it before I was able to stagger out upon the beach and fall to the dry sand in safety.

There I lay for as much as five minutes, sobbing for breath, and utterly spent, while old Tom, who had followed me, sprawled out near by.

Being young, my laboring heart slowed down to its normal pace before Tom was able to speak, and I sat up. To my consternation, I saw that the gig was dragging her anchor!

I didn't tell Tom at once. I just dropped back on the sand

and stared at the stars. For a space I lay there, crushed by defeat. I didn't want to watch that boat breaking up, nor to see those precious stores swept away into the undertow.

It was Tom who spoke first. He raised his head, saw what was impending, and groaned. He flopped back on the sands.

"I knew it," he said, as though he were speaking to himself. "The devil's with him, and you may lay to it."

In another minute I had regained a bit of spirit. At least, I thought, I might as well play the hideous nightmare out to the end; and I arose, thinking that I would attempt to save some of the stores and arms when she struck.

"What it is to be young!" sighed old Tom, struggling up to follow me.

Half filled with water as she was, at the last, one great comber picked the gig up, turned her completely over, dumped all the stores overboard and dropped her, bottom up, on the sands. She was not in danger now of breaking up, it was true, but how could we ever put to sea without stores?

We did not lose everything. At the risk of being sucked outward by the undertow we retrieved five oars, three muskets, and one-small barrel of pork. The water cask, the powder and all the remaining cargo were hopelessly scattered.

"The tide has still a ways to go out," said Tom, "and maybe we'll find some of the stuff. But I ain't got much hope."

Neither had I. Nevertheless I was already determined on at least one more move before we gave up.

"Either," said I, "our party was lost for a time in the dark, or they were laid by the heels. I've got to find out."

Old Tom argued that surely the captain's party had only been delayed by their wounded, and their unfamiliarity with the terrain, and would shortly appear upon the beach. He contended that they might have been forced to take a circuitous route which would bring them out on the eastern coast of the island at a point north of our landing place.

"In that case," I argued, "it'll be best for you to beat up the beach. If you get in touch with them, and the surf dies down with the turn in the tide, make for the ship. And if I see no signs of them at the stockade I'll work down along the east side of the harbor to the schooner."

To this Tom reluctantly agreed. "Just help me right her, lad, and then go ahead," said he. "We've had such rotten luck that I ain't the one to say no to anything no more."

So, the tide receding further, we managed to right the gig, and I tightened my belt and started.

# 28

## A BOLD MOVE

**NOTHING OCCURRED TO** delay me, and I came to the western shore of Hangman's Bay, at a point near the north or blockhouse end of the harbor, just as the first light of a dawning day began to disperse the shadows. And there, on the bosom of the bay, returning from south'ard, was the *Vulture's* jolly boat!

"They've been down to the passage and discovered the schooner," was my first sickening thought.

Four people were manning the oars. As they came closer I recognized Dick, that bold wench Belle Saunders, and two of the buccaneers.

The trees grew close to the high-water mark along this part of the harbor, and extended along the north shore to the corner of the clearing. Well screened from the pirates' view, I was crouching behind some bushes before their prow grounded.

Before they reached shore, I saw Beau Tyron approach the water's edge, within a stone's toss of my hiding-place.

Dick and his small crew were rowing swiftly. I could see that all were elated; yet there was something odd and secretive in their manner, too. It seemed to me that they should have been shouting the glad news to their comrades before this—had they discovered the ship.

The explanation came quickly enough. When they landed, out jumped Dick, leaving the other three to haul up the jolly boat.

"Did you have any luck?" Dick asked eagerly.

"No," said Tyron, and cursed. "We went clear through to the east shore and back again. Never saw a sign of them."

"They must be hiding somewhere, then, atween here and the east coast," said Dick. He was speaking in lowered tones, and glancing at the stockade. "Tell me," Dick hurried on, "are those swabs asleep?"

"Asleep, and drunk!" Tyron returned, surlily. He quickened at something in Dick's manner, and cried, "Why do you reason Captain Fogg's party is on Kidd's Neck? The ship should have been around by the time we got to the east coast, but she wasn't in sight. We reasoned that they must mean to board her over on the west coast. At Execution Inlet, for instance."

"And if that had been the case, they'd have been aboard by now!" said Dick. He stood there for a moment, eying Tyron thoughtfully. I knew he was weighing Tyron in the balance. Something of this must have been sensed by the Britisher, too, for he fidgeted nervously and drew back, his hand hovering close to the butt of a pistol which he had thrust into his belt. He watched Dick as a cornered rat watches a cat.

The other three came up, in the meantime, and Belle sidled close to Dick, her hand clapped on a pistol butt. They remained thus during a tense instant, Dick's eyes narrowed to slits.

"By the devil," Tyron suddenly exploded, "I believe you've found that the schooner came a cropper on a sand-bar in the passage!"

"So?" said Dick. "Well, not so loud or it'll be the worse for you."

"Best give him a dose of lead, and be done with it!" said Belle. "Didn't he swing along with Hardy trying to depose you last night?"

DICK SLOWLY SHOOK his head. He had made his decision. "Killing him would maybe start a ruckus to spoil it all," he said, "and he's too smart to fool, I take it." To Tyron he continued:

"You're after that girl, and that girl you'll have, come hell or high water. Last night you were about to swing with Hardy. Well, you've seen how he and his mess o' swabs stack up, for sand and headwork. So you can cast your lot right now, you can—and if you wants that girl, you'll cast it with me."

"You mean you've got her?" Tyron cried excitedly.

"Take a reef in that jaw tackle!" Dick warned fiercely. "No, I ain't got her. I've got the ship, though. There's a point, you'll grant. You can't get the girl off this island without no ship, my hearty."

Tyron cleared his throat. "You've got that ship aground in the channel!" he hoarsely asserted. "One word from me to Hardy—"

"Ah, finish him, Dick!" Belle pleaded.

Again Dick shook his bandaged head. "Well," said he, "supposin' we have found her so? Just supposin' we lets you live long enough to warn Hardy—what'll you gain? Hardy can't navigate, and you know it."

Tyron cursed under his breath.

"On the other hand," Dick continued, "if you want to throw in with us, I'll give you my affy-davy, I will. Once we're afloat we'll bargain for that girl."

"How?"

"How? Why, Hardy and his troublemakers will be left ashore here with neither boat nor much in the way of stores, won't they? I reckon they'll be open to reason. Aye, they'll overhaul this island from stem to stern to find that girl, and you may lay to it. I'll trade 'em a gig and stores for that girl, and stand off and on till they gets her."

I think that the wretched Tyron was at his wit's end. Upon the altar of a mad love he had sacrificed his last shreds of honor. He was, in truth, a pitiable figure, shorn of his nonchalance, shorn of his foppish *savoir-faire*, shorn of all the priceless reserve supplies which more honorable men store up in their mental lockers to draw upon in times of stress.

"I'll close with you on that," he said. "What I don't see, though, is how you'll manage—"

"You'll see soon enough," Dick interrupted, with some impatience. And they started up the beach toward the blockhouse, talking in a low tone.

My best course at this juncture was a grim puzzle. I saw no reason to doubt Tyron's version of the pursuit. The captain's party had eluded him. This, I reasoned, accounted for their delay; quite possibly the party had been forced to hide in the woods till certain that the coast was clear. If they had not already joined with Tom Newgate it was reasonable to believe that they would shortly come up with him, and, the surf permitting, put to sea in the gig and row down to the schooner.

I reckoned that at least four hours or more must pass before the incoming tide was high enough to enable my friends to work the *Bonny Lee* off the spit. If I proceeded at once to the schooner I could be of little aid to them till the tide rose.

What I had just overheard further influenced me. It seemed unlikely that Dick had left a watchman on the schooner. He would not want to rouse suspicion by leaving behind him one of the small crew which had set out with him in the jolly boat.

"Moreover, the schooner is hard and fast," I reasoned, "and, the gig being gone, he thinks that Tom and I have given up the idea of refloating the ship, and are taking our chances at sea in the open boat."

THE MORE I turned these things over in my mind, the stronger became my determination to remain near the stockade for the present. While there I could keep an eye on developments.

Just how Dick intended to effect his object I had no means of knowing. Nor was it made more clear to me when I noted the next move. Dick and his four companions reached the blockhouse; I saw that a few of the drowsy buccaneers roused to question them; and after a parley which I could not overhear at that distance, Dick, accompanied by Belle Saunders, Beau Tyron, and the ruffian known as Bill, set out to north'ard. They crossed the paling and disappeared in the trees which covered the slopes under the shadow of Tops'l Hill.

The sun was well up, and more than three hours went by

before my patience was rewarded. During this time only a few buccaneers moved into my sight, on the knoll, and these talked in low tones, lest they waken their comrades who were still lost in slumber—the pirates fogged with rum, and the prisoners weighed down by fatigue. Then, in a jiffy, the whole camp was aroused by the return of Tiger Dick.

The pirate chieftain and his three companions came hurriedly out of the woods to north'ard, as though afire with excitement. Dick, I noticed, was limping; his right ankle appeared to have been sprained, and he used a stick as a cane to ease the strain of each painful step. "Stand to, all-l-ll hands!" bawled the pirate Bill. *"We've found the ship."*

The cry brought the pirates out of the blockhouse on the run. Dick coming over the paling awkwardly, they crowded round him, all clamoring at once till he silenced them with a gesture and pointed westward.

"Over there in Execution Inlet, like Bill told you!" he cried. "Did you think I'd be drowning my troubles in rum, and letting them get clean away, like you? Ah, I'd be dancing a hornpipe in a rope's end at Execution Dock if I left things to you, by the powers! Well, I laid aloft on old Tops'l Hill, I did, and got this here sprained ankle, damn it! But I see that ship, beached in Execution Inlet."

"Beached?" cried Hardy Flintlock.

"Why would they beach her?"

"Why?" roared Dick. "I suppose they did it on purpose, you wooden-headed lubber! Bill here told you there was only two boarded her when that swab Morrison—damn him!—tried to knife him, and lost us our ship, by thunder. Maybe Tom Newgate run her aground to careen!" And at this sarcastic sally some of the listeners broke out with guffaws.

"Well, I was wondering why they didn't stand off and on and put off that gig to take their friends aboard," Hardy growled.

"In the surf?" cried Dick. "Ah, but if you'd stirred your stumps, and gone aloft with us, instead of sleeping off your rum, you'd have seen that surf, you would. Anyways, they put into Execution Inlet to take their party aboard—and came a cropper. There she lays, heeled over on her beam ends. It looks from here as though they couldn't no ways float her without a full crew at the capstan to haul her off the bar. That's where you come in. Don't stand there, but shake a leg."

"To row round there?" Hardy cried.

"Row? Who said row? You'll take all hands, but a few to stay with me, and go straight overland, my hearty. You know the trail, I reckon. It's miles shorter than going round by boat. Get your breakfasts in your fists, and bundle out of here, my lads. Bundle out of this while you've a chance to run out along that bar and lay them lubbers aboard."

HE FAIRLY SHOVED the men before him toward the blockhouse and they piled within. Sounds of hurry reached me, and now and then a phrase from the babble of voices; but within a few minutes Hardy Flintlock emerged at the head of a dozen or more men. Several of these were bandaged, but were ordered along with the rest.

Carrying two muskets apiece, slung behind their broad backs, and armed with cutlasses and pistols, these growling pirates went over the paling and were soon hidden from view in the forest to westward.

Dick's strategy was plain enough to me by now. He had sent the dupes on a wild goose chase to the west coast, retaining with him Beau Tyron, Belle Saunders, and the half dozen hands who had remained faithful to him in that election the night before. By the time Hardy discovered the truth Dick meant to be standing off to sea in the *Bonny Lee*.

The conspirators waited only long enough to be certain that Hardy and his men were well away. Assured of this, Dick called the prisoners from their breakfast and set them to carrying the chests of gold to the gig and jolly boat. His lameness had been but a sham, to account for his not accompanying Hardy and the rest.

They would soon be under way, at this rate, and I darted back into the brush, and started southward to warn my friends; for, if the surf had lessened, they had been enabled to launch the gig, I reasoned. In that case they must have reached the *Bonny Lee,* and might be caught by these inhuman devils before they could put themselves into position for a strong defense.

Taking care to keep out of sight in the forest, I ran the greater part of the three miles to southward, only slowing to a rapid walk now and then to regain lost breath. Occasionally I edged close to the beach to look backward at the buccaneers, and when I was near the entrance of the passageway, saw that they had embarked. By the flash of the oars I knew that they had not left the prisoners behind, but had brought them along to work the ship off.

Well-nigh breathless, I took another hitch in my belt and increased my speed. It occurred to me that surely the captain would have placed a sentry near the entrance to watch the upper harbor, had his party regained the ship.

I saw no signs of any one. Nor were there signs of life on the schooner when I doubled round the twisting turns and came at last in sight of her.

She lay as we had left her, her nose embedded in the sandy bar, and her stern afloat. There was only this difference: the tide had turned, and had risen sufficiently for Dick's men to work her off in a brace of shakes.

"That cursed surf," I thought, "has kept our party from putting off in the gig!"

# 29

## THE COURAGE OF DESPERATION

**I WAS NEVER** so near to wringing my hands like a helpless, distracted woman. My head hung listlessly and my hands dangled like weights.

Then, even as I was plunged into the depths of hopeless despair, I heard a sound; and the sound was that of oars!

I raised my head, as a startled stag whips up his antlers when alarmed. I drew a whistling breath; new life pulsed through me; and how I ran toward that bend to southward!

My friends were there, in the gig—my poor, forlorn, and almost hopeless comrades, playing this game of life and death to the end. How gaunt and weary and hollow-eyed they were! How gray their faces, how blue their lips, and how dark their tired eyes!

They needed not to tell me of their travails in floundering through the woods; they needed not to tell me of the fearful struggle they had had to launch the heavy gig in combers that abated only slightly after I left Tom on the coast.

They had been swamped time and again before they finally succeeded in getting off, as I learned later; but I could have guessed this by one look at their faces.

In view of this, the thought that popped into my mind

then was apparently born of lunacy. Yet it seemed to me that we must make one more final, desperate effort if we were to win freedom and save our lives. As I beckoned to them, and they pointed the nose of the gig ashore, I began to talk.

They said never a word at first, either in way of greeting or comment. They were too tired, and were also well-nigh stunned by the news that the buccaneers under Dick were coming down the bay to take the ship.

"They'll be twenty-five minutes or more pulling down here against the tide," I cried, "and we can be aboard that schooner in two shakes of a lamb's tail, I tell you!"

"You mean to fight them, my lad?" the captain asked, dully.

"No, no, no!" I cried, with a sob in my voice. My nerves were on edge, as the saying goes; my words tumbled over one another. A scarecrow on my own account and my head encircled by a bloody bandage, I croaked like a raven at these wan, blood-stained scarecrows in the gig, striving to rouse them.

"If we fight them now," I declared, "we can stave off Dick and his half dozen rascals—but how will we work off the ship? And we'll have Hardy and his crew from the west side about our ears before we are through with it."

"Then what do you propose?"

"Why, to lay aboard, and hide in the lazaret, till they've worked her off. Then we can lay Dick's men athwart—and God defend the right!"

**MULLINS AND TRAYNOR** groaned hopelessly. It was madness, Traynor whispered. We had better turn and put to sea in the gig before Dick came in sight. But Gwendolyn roused and cried, "We'll go aboard!" And the skipper, coming to his feet with a mighty lurch, settled the matter.

"Out of this gig, my lads!" he ordered—and he looked like a skeleton covered with pale skin, as he barked the command. A skeleton save for his eyes—and these had lighted with a blaze that fairly scorched the fainthearted among us.

"Hide the gig in the bushes!" he next ordered. "If they see her, they'll guess the truth, and all's up."

How some of that crew managed to pull, I cannot tell you. But pull we did, and into the bushes shot the gig. That done, we hastened to the near-by sandspit, waded out to the bows of the *Bonny Lee*, and began laying aboard by way of the martingales.

The lazaret lay aft, under the cabin. Into this storeroom we piled, one after another and closed the hatch above our heads. There we crouched in semidarkness, waiting for Dick and his crew to come aboard.

We were risking all on a throw of the dice. If the buccaneers opened the hatch over our heads, we were lost. We would be shot down before we could gain the upper deck.

Even if we were not discovered, we must be reasonably certain of our enemies' positions before we fell upon them. We had Tiger Dick, Belle Saunders and six strong and ruthless buccaneers to contend with. Only Tom Newgate, Abe Kemp and myself were able to move about in able-bodied fashion; the others were handicapped in their movements by grievous injuries, and would be of aid to us only if they were fortunate enough to get into position for pistol fire.

"There's the chief rub," said the skipper, looking round

a white-faced circle that was busily engaged in examining primings. "We don't know how many will remain in the cabin after they get the ship afloat. Maybe none will while they're sailing down the passage. But we don't know. And we can't be popping up through that hatchway while one of those devils holds the cabin. So I've got to send one of you forward."

We stared at him. "What for, sir?" asked Abe Kemp.

"To seize a chance to create some kind of disturbance at the right moment!" snapped the desperate skipper. "I don't care what—but something. He's got to lay low, and keep his ears open, and use his head. And Ned Allen's the man for it, by thunder! Ned, I bank on you. What in the devil to tell you to do, I don't know—but you'll think of something."

If he had asked me what I intended to do, I could not have answered. Yet go I must; and likewise must I hit upon some device to bring the pirates forward, giving my friends a chance to pop out into the cabin.

The responsibility almost overwhelmed me. "Captain," I cried, "my head aches! Can't some of you think of something I can do up forward?"

"A fire!" said Gwendolyn, instantly. "Here, take this flint and tinder."

I seized it eagerly. "It's the very thing!" exclaimed the captain. "By gum, they'll be above decks while they're going down the passage, I'll gamble. That's the dodge. Lay forward, now, my lad—and God bless you!"

I gained the fo'c's'le a bare moment or two before the pirates and their wretched prisoners appeared astern.

# 30

## A FATEFUL CHOICE

**BEFORE I HAD** been in the fo'c's'le more than a few seconds I saw that I would have to abandon the plan to start a smudge. I found only a few old shirts and other bits of clothing, and not even so much as a bit of oakum to start a blaze.

I next thought of entering the locker room, where oils and oakum were stored. I found this to be locked. A quick trip to the galley proved that this was barren of shavings, and I had to whisk back into the fo'c's'le as Dick and his crew came alongside.

"Lay aboard with that blunt, and lively!" I heard Dick ordering. "And, Bill, you take four hands and get a line ashore."

Next I heard his voice on deck, hurrying the laboring prisoners who were coming up the gangway with the chests of gold in their tired arms.

I crouched there, near the companionway, pistols in hand. No one approached the fo'c's'le immediately, however, and I breathed more easily. The gold, as we had reasoned, was being carried aft to the cabin.

The fo'c's'le in the *Bonny Lee* had been divided into sleeping quarters, for the hands before the mast, on the port side, the locker and sail rooms taking up the starboard side. A triple tier of bunks, with sides at least a foot in height, had been built to port; and near the head of the last upper bunk aft was a porthole for light and air. I decided to take advantage of this to get the lay of the land.

Accordingly I crawled into the upper bunk in question, and leaned from it just far enough to peer cautiously past the edge of the porthole.

From this position I could see the length of the ship. I could also see the pirate, Bill, who had pulled ashore in the jolly boat, and was directing the efforts of four prisoners, now busily engaged in fastening a line to a tree. The tree was on a point, directly astern of the ship, and the line trailed through the water to the stern.

Tiger Dick stood near the taffrail. Now he said a word to the prisoners who disappeared down the companionway, carrying the brass-bound chests; now he spoke to the hairy pirate who was busy with a coil at the end of the line; and again he called out a low but clear order to another buccaneer who, with four captives, came forward to mount the fo'c's'le deck, above my head.

These prisoners, their jangling chains brought up from their ankle irons over one shoulder, and carrying the ten-pound iron balls against their backs, were immediately busy at the capstan. In a trice they were running a line aft along the deck. All this while, Beau Tyron lounged against the bulwarks on the port side of the waist, keeping a sour eye on the British tars who carried the chests up the gangway from the gig. His red-rimmed eyes, his stubble of beard, and his disgruntled, embittered expression spoke eloquently of his caliber in adversity.

**THEY WERE NOT** long about their business. The chests were soon stowed below; the lines were made fast; and as Belle came out of the cabin, all hands aboard ship were bundled forward to man the capstan bars.

For safety's sake I deserted the porthole and lay flat in the berth. But I could hear them, overhead. Bill and his four prisoners had returned aboard to swell the numbers, and in a moment the fourteen captives and the half dozen buccaneers were heaving away lustily.

I heard the capstan creak and groan; the line thrummed and hummed; and the schooner budged a bit in the mud. But another, and still another heave failed to move her.

"Ease up, my lads!" said Dick, quite undismayed. "Lay below, and fetch out block and falls."

Down they came tumbling into the fo'c's'le, while I crouched flat in the bunk. They hurried into the locker room and shortly returned on deck dragging a heavy set of blocks and falls.

"Bill," I heard Dick say next, "take three of your own messmates with you ashore—and four of these gentlemen in irons to man oars."

While this order was being obeyed, Dick told the prisoners around the capstan that they might rest, and he and Belle Saunders went aft to the waist, leaving one buccaneer on guard forward. Again I sought the porthole, in hopes that I might find the after part of the ship deserted.

In this I was disappointed, for the great hairy buccaneer was near the taffrail, making ready to fasten one end of the blocks.

In the interim, Tiger Dick had paused to raise one foot

to a gun carriage, on the port side, and was polishing the silver buckle of his shoe with a kerchief!

"What a man!" cried Belle Saunders, teasingly. "I do believe you'd stop to tidy yourself in a hurricane. And you men say that women are vain!"

He smiled at her, caressingly. It transformed his face. Throwing one arm around her supple waist, he gave to the buckle one last touch, stood erect, and drew her close. It was a gentle gesture, too.

"Why shouldn't I be vain," he returned, "after winning the finest woman on God's footstool?"

The warm, rich color tinted her smooth cheeks, and her firm breasts rose and trembled with her deep breath. A tremor of happiness shook her. Her heavy, waving tresses were unbound and falling in abandon over her shoulders; they gleamed in the sun like strands of red gold, with the warm tints of autumn leaves in the hollows; and her red, red mouth was warm and sweet, and her eyes were brimming with tenderness.

"Dick," she murmured. "Dick!"

Then she stirred, and her brows wrinkled apprehensively. "Hadn't you better hurry them?" she suggested, looking westward, where Hardy and his mates were presumably trudging toward Execution Inlet.

"YOU MEAN BILL?" said he. "Why, honey, Bill is mate now. He's a handy mate, too, never fear. As for Hardy—that swab is not going to trouble us any more."

"I hope not," she said, sighing. And she blushed. "I—I never felt like this, Dick. I'm nervous. I want to get away. And it isn't the money, Dick, either. I'm not afraid we'll lose the money. I'm afraid something will happen to you."

He laughed low, and indulgently. This man who would crush all who stood in his path as ruthlessly as a man crushes an insect under the ball of his thumb, now gave her shoulder an affectionate pat.

"Nothing will happen to me, girl. But I know how you feel. I—why, burn me, I don't care half so much about that blunt as I thought I did. If—well, what I mean is this: I've fought, and I've risked swinging, and I've cut down men like so many beeves, to get that blunt. Now, if it came to a choice between you and those doubloons, why—by thunder!—I'd take you."

"Ah, but you don't mean that!" she cried, her face radiant.

A new voice cut in on them here. It was that of Beau Tyron.

"I think," he said, sarcastically, "that you'd best have him put that in writing, Miss Saunders."

Dick dropped his arm from Belle's waist, and whirled.

"Ha!" he cried. "You're still harping on that strain, milord. By George, if I hadn't given you my word, I'd settle you out of hand."

Tyron laughed hollowly. Either he regained a bit of his old spirit, or he dared Fate with the recklessness of a man whose mouth tastes the bitter ashes of despair.

"You gave me your word you'd force them to hunt for Miss Leigh," said he. "That's true. Now that she's put to sea in the gig, I suppose I can whistle for my bargain."

"Why, we'll overhaul them, one way or another."

"You mean you'll beat up the wind till we sight 'em?" cried Tyron incredulously.

"A bargain's a bargain," Dick returned.

Tyron stared. "So it is," he replied slowly. "So it is. Only—what sort of bargain have you kept with Hardy Flintlock?"

The blood thickened in Dick's cheeks. "Damn you," he cried hoarsely, "I've had enough of this. It's them that broke the bargain, setting out to depose me. You take a reef in your jaw tackle, and let me hear no more of bargains till I've broken one with you."

All this while I was thinking swiftly. Sooner or later I must act—and when Tyron glared and turned away toward the bulwarks, I decided that no better opportunity would present itself.

The prisoners, I reasoned, would either stay quiet, or jump in to help us. For had not Captain Fogg protected them from the wrath of the released convicts? Those British salts would undoubtedly prefer us as captors.

So thinking, I drew a great breath, looked to my priming, then slipped out of the berth and sought the companionway.

**CAUTIOUSLY I RAISED** my head till I could again survey the upper deck. Belle and Dick had moved over to the starboard side, and Belle was seated on the bulwarks. Between my position and theirs was a yawning, open hatchway in the upper deck. Beau Tyron was on the port side, somewhat aft of this hatchway. The hairy felon's head and shoulders projected above the line of the cabin roof, astern.

My first intentions were to take careful aim and shoot this fellow through the back. But as I raised my pistol my heart failed me. Something within me revolted against the act. I aimed at his arm instead and pulled the trigger.

The report crashed and reverberated within the fo'c's'le like the roar of a cannon. And the bearded pirate leaped and howled in pain and rage. My bullet had whipped across the deck and struck him fair in the right arm.

Quick as thought I leaped on deck. In my hands I carried two doublebarreled pistols. Three shots remained in my locker. I aimed this time at Tiger Dick and fired again.

I had hoped that the hairy fellow would either be downed, and helpless with pain, or that he would rush forward to aid Dick. But the very eagerness of my friends to join forces with me frustrated their own ends.

Just before I pulled trigger the second time I heard the hatchway crash open, in the after cabin, and the fellow with the thick beard whipped up a pistol and fired down the companionway.

"I've got 'em bottled!" he roared, letting fly with another barrel. Though one arm was shattered, this man was no coward, and he stood there like a bloody Spartan, armed with a fresh pistol which he had jerked from his sash, and now had cocked and ready to fire again at the first head that appeared.

While this went on, there was a commotion on the fo'c's'le deck. Some of the British prisoners had leaped for the sentry there. His pistol barked once, and again. There was a scream of pain, and a heavy fall. Close upon this came a crash and the sickening thud of iron balls wielded as bludgeons to beat the pirate to the deck.

This came to me as the acrid smoke drifted up from my hot pistol muzzle, and I realized that I had missed; for Dick jerked two pistols free from the bandolier across his broad, curved breast, and raised one weapon in his right hand.

The clap of its report fell close upon the roar of my own

weapon. I received a sledgehammer blow in the upper left breast and went down in a heap on the planks.

I fell on my side. My pistols dropped from nerveless fingers. Blood filled my mouth, but I did not lose consciousness. The frightful pain seemed rather to clear my head than to set me swooning.

Vainly I tried to summon strength to reach my loaded pistol. It lay on the deck not more than a foot from my outstretched hand. I could not push my hand out more than an inch or two. And there I lay, quivering and helpless, but strangely clear of mind and eye while destiny hung in the balance.

**DICK GAVE ME** but one flashing glance, for three raging British tars were leaping from the fo'c's'le deck to come at him with their murderous iron balls.

Belle Saunders, at this juncture, was still seated on the starboard bulwarks. She had twisted on her hips and had jerked out a pistol, when old Tom Newgate, with a cutlass in his teeth, popped his head up above the edge of the open hatchway in the upper deck, between Dick and the onrushing British tars.

And that was the situation when Beau Tyron entered the lists. He was still on the port side of the ship. He must have believed that this was a golden opportunity to turn the tide against the buccaneers, and, by so doing, wipe out Gwendolyn's memory of his duplicity and treachery. Sick minds grasp at straws. At all events he lifted his arm and sighted a pistol at Tiger Dick's profile.

Dick's weapon belched flame and smoke, the first of the three prisoners screeched in dire pain, and fell with a shattered shoulder to the planking. His comrades whipped about and plunged head foremost into the companionway.

Belle's shot split the echo of Dick's report, and another prisoner on the fo'c's'le deck groaned horribly. His mates were scurrying like frightened rabbits for the cover afforded by bitts and capstan when Tyron's treacherous pistol thundered from the port side of the schooner.

The bullet missed Dick narrowly. But it found a target in the pistol which Belle held in her hand. The weapon was whipped from her grasp, and, taken by surprise, and jarred by the smashing blow, Belle lost her balance. With a startled cry she fell backward and plunged downward toward the water.

Before she struck, Dick had fired his second barrel at Tom Newgate. The leaden slug smashed into Tom's cutlass blade, close to his jaw. He was knocked backward, end over end, into the hold, even while Dick was grasping the significance of the attack from his flank.

He dodged as Tyron pulled trigger again and missed fire; and before the cursing, snarling wretch could present another pistol Dick pulled a fresh weapon from his bandolier and shot Tyron through the heart.

With a sound that was like a sob, Dick ground out an oath and leaped to the bulwarks. I could hear Belle floundering in the water.

"Are you hurt, girl?" he called anxiously, one eye flitting back over his shoulder to watch the open hatchway. His face was gray. "Ah! Then, if you're not, why don't you swim round the stern to the gangway?"

Below, in the water, the struggling woman must have misled him for the moment, must have given him the impression that she was at home in the water. It was only for a second. No seasoned swimmer flounders so noisily. She suddenly cried out in fear:

"A line, Dick! A line! I can't—I can't swim."

**HIS EYES DARTED** feverishly here and there. A loose line lay coiled near the mainmast. He darted toward it and scooped it up. Over the side it went, like a hissing snake, while below decks in the passageway, I heard the sound of running feet.

"God!" cried Dick. And I knew that Belle had missed the rope, and was sinking.

It was there that Dick faced the crisis of his career. His restless spirit had rebelled against the commonplace life in which meeker souls are drugged by the monotony of ordinary events; and money—"the blunt"—had been his god.

Not even now did he make his decision without a fearful struggle. He had us on the hip, and he knew it. The hairy pirate commanded the hatchway in the floor of the after cabin. Bill and his three buccaneer mates were falling into the jolly boat to come back aboard. No man could thrust his head up through the hatchway in the waist, amidships, and live.

Dick had but to remain there, guarding it, till Bill and the other three came over the side, and the day was won.

But he hesitated not more than a second or two. With a choked cry he cast everything to the four winds, jumped to the bulwarks and shot outward and downward in a magnificent dive.

"The fool, the fool, the damned crazy fool!" howled the bearded pirate. "Row, Bill—hurry!"

I made one last dying effort—for dying I believed myself

to be. I reached the pistol, lifted it, and fired at the fellow abaft the cabin. Flying splinters made him dodge, and then Tom Newgate—whom I had thought dead—came out of the hatchway amidships. He was followed by Gwendolyn and Mullins.

As in a dream I managed to reach my feet. I heard their pistols exploding, and other shots from the interior of the cabin. I knew that the remainder of my friends were coming up through the hatchway from the lazaret.

With Mullins and Tom Newgate running aft along the deck, and firing as they went, and Traynor, Digby, and the skipper shooting from the lazaret hatch, the last buccaneer aboard ship saw the writing on the wall. He fired hastily, but this was in the act of vaulting the taffrail.

His plunge into the water cleared the deck. We had the ship.

More shots came from astern as my friends pumped lead at Bill and his mates in the jolly boat. These saw that the game was up, and in their haste to abandon the boat and save their skins they nearly upset her. They leaped into the shallow water, scrambled for the near-by shore, and whisked out of sight in the brush, in a panic of fear.

I staggered to the bulwarks, on the starboard side. My heart was afire with the lust for retribution. With my last ounce of strength I intended to fire my final shot and send Dick down to join those unfortunates whom he had consigned so callously to the locker of Davy Jones.

**IT WAS AT** the bulwarks that I saw the truth. Dick was struggling in the water, not more than a half dozen feet from the side of the hull. Belle was tightly held in the crook of his great left arm. But both were drowning. With all his strength, Dick was in the same boat with thousands of other men who have lived their lives upon the sea: for he could barely swim!

Yet, knowing that, he went over after her anyway!

Dick's face was purple with his struggles. He was trying to reach the line which he had thrown to Belle. Now it dangled from the bulwarks to the water's edge, snug beside the planking of the ship.

He looked up. By not so much as a contraction of the eyes did he show fear. The very manner in which he flung up his chin defied me to do my worst.

It was that, I think, that stayed my trigger finger. I learned a great truth, too—that when one is close to death, as I was, hatreds and the lust for retribution fade into the insignificance of unrealities. My pistol dropped from my hand.

At that, Dick's outstretched hand caught the dangling line, and Mullins came running to the ship's side with a cannon ball which he had retrieved from the scuppers. He raised it to drop down on Dick's head. But I had strength enough to lurch against him, and the man's aim was spoiled.

I was falling to the deck, in a half swoon. But things did not go completely black till I had heard Cap'n Fogg shouting, "Drop it, Mullins, drop it!" The man, it appeared, had grabbed up another cannon ball. "We've not got to the point, by hickory, where we'll murder those who can't hit back!" the skipper roared.

# 31

## FAIR WEATHER

**WHEN I REGAINED** my senses I was lying in a berth in the after cabin. It was well along in the afternoon, and we were standing out to sea.

Gwendolyn sat beside me—a figure at first misty, then more and more clear to my eyes.

"Do you know me?" she asked.

I nodded and struggled to separate the first dreamy impressions from the real. "You've been kissing me!" I charged.

Her face flamed rosily. "You mustn't talk!" she cried, hastily, jumping up. "Captain!" she called, excitedly, "he's awake, he's awake!"

The door of the little stateroom flew open and there was the skipper and Tom Newgate, with Abe Kemp just behind them. What a permanent place each one had carved for himself within my heart! Their eyes were misty, and one and all had a word of thankfulness to say for my apparent chances of recovery. For while I had been shot through the body, the bullet had not touched the lung, and with my youth and physique to aid me, only rest was needed to put me on my feet again.

They were so confounded exclamatory, and so happy

over my escape from death, and so relieved and buoyed by the sunshine which had at last appeared from behind the black clouds on our horizon, that it was some minutes before I could get from them a coherent account of the events following my lapse into oblivion.

Then I learned that Dick and Belle still lived! Our skipper had dropped over a plank to aid Dick in swimming ashore. After which the British tars were ordered to heave at the line and work off the ship.

"Willing enough they were, too," said the skipper. "Some mighty fine chaps among them, I tell you. They could have been pirates themselves, you remember, but wouldn't. I'm glad to think we saved the best of 'em."

I was equally glad, and said as much; but, despite all the evil of his ways, I felt somewhat sorry for Dick Buntline.

"He'll have short shrift when Hardy and his rascals come back from the west shore," I remarked.

They all smiled, and Tom raised my head so I might look out of a porthole. Far away on the bosom of the glimmering sea I saw a small boat, under a sprits'l.

"I wouldn't make a good judge, I reckon," said the skipper, smiling ruefully. "That's Dick, and Belle, and the messmates who were loyal to him. I gave 'em the gig we left in the bushes. Likewise some stores—and a chest full of those doubloons. They might have killed some of us from behind the trees—for they had a few shots left, d'y'see. As for Hardy and his cutthroats, they can stay on that island till they rot, for all of me."

And then he bundled the happy lot from the stateroom, leaving Gwendolyn to face the music.

"You must go to sleep!" she commanded, rosily.

"Not," said I, "till you put on that ball and chain!"

"I won't!" she cried, her cheeks aflame. "I won't say, 'I'll obey!' to any man. I won't, I won't—"

But she did, for I had strength enough to raise my hand to the back of her head; and then, with a smothered cry, she kissed me, not once, but over and over again.

And so the captain married us, and so we sailed away in happiness from that tragic island in the southern sea.

**WE HAD NO** trouble with the British tars. Coffin, Kemp and Tom Newgate acted as mates.

Cap'n Fogg and our wounded shipmates mended rapidly; and we had come to an agreement with our British prisoners which did away with the fear of further trouble. We were to cruise about till our own hands were sufficiently recovered to work the ship, and then the Britishers were to be set ashore on one of the Bahamas, with two hundred pounds apiece.

"That," said one of them, "is more than handsome. We couldn't expect anything fairer than that from our own folks!"

But before that happened, we heard a piece of news which mightily relieved our minds. In effect, if not by deliberate intention, we were pirates in the eyes of British law. It is therefore easy to imagine our relief and joy when we sighted a Yankee schooner which told us that the colonies were up in arms.

"Then we're not outlaws, but rebels, by thunder!" said the skipper. "And thank God for that!"

How we ran the blockade, landed on a lonely part of the Carolina coast, buried the treasure, and came back overland to retrieve it later, is another story. All surviving hands shared in the division, and after my part in the Revolution, I recovered my father's estate. There Gwendolyn and I settled down, and there Cap'n Fogg and Abe Kemp came more than once to visit us. As for Tom Newgate, a little shop is what he wanted, and a little shop is what Tom built. There he makes toy ships and windmills for my oldest boy, and shifts his quid from side to side, and is content.

None of us ever saw Tiger Dick again. Abe Kemp rose to a captaincy at sea, and eventually ran across the man called Bill, in Port o' Spain. Bill told him that the gig reached Havana safely, and that Dick and Belle planned to start a plantation near there.

I had no quarrel to pick with this; in fact, whenever the notion took me to smell the salt again, and we went for a voyage at sea, I never sighted a tops'l on the horizon without wondering what would happen if Tiger Dick were aboard the stranger.

As I think of it all and hold my dear wife close in the crook of my arm, I realize that I have much to thank Dick for. Had it not been for him the *Bonny Lee* would not have steered for Camano Island to calk that leak; and in that case I would never have met up with a loyal, fiery, loving mate who is far more precious to me than all of Tiger Dick's doubloons.

# THE MEN WHO MAKE THE
# ARGOSY: DON McGREW

*Author of "Alexander the Red," "The Masked*
*Barmaid," "Tiger Dick's Doubloons," etc.*

**THE MAN BEHIND** the Big Desk has asked me to do various and divers things with the pronoun I. And what a dreadful task that is for writers and members of the Lambs Club!

Indiana is my native State; and though once upon a time I lived in Bagdad-on-the-Hudson, and tried to hide the earmarks behind a cane, spats and a Homburg hat, some butter and egg waif from Logansport, Fort Wayne, or Hagerstown would invariably pierce through my disguise, to the Hoosier core of me, and call upon me, as a fellow lodge member, in moments of distress. The Hoosier stamp is always recognizable. In my peregrinations over the seven seas I have never been able to fool any one of discernment: once a Hoosier, always a Hoosier.

My activities? A soldier in the regular cavalry, in Mindanao—Mexican Border service in the Second Maine Infantry—a dispensable lieutenant commanding a one pound gun platoon with the 103rd Infantry, 26th Division, in France—newspaper experience from reporter

to managing editor—a
young cub who, at the
age of nineteen, wrote
a story in the Philip-
pines, and subsequently
sold it to the late Charles
Agnew MacLean—that,
I think, touches some of
the high lights. I have
been hither and yon, and
up and down the face
of the earth, and have
finally cast anchor in

Seattle where God rested—according to our Chamber of
Commerce—after giving mere routine attention to the
formation of other spots on this mudball.

Likes? Above all, active, thinking, observant people,
who, in their travels and occupations have been constantly
athirst for added knowledge. My favorite game is *chong
ki*—though Dr. Lasker, Anderssen and Zukertort called
it chess. But, to offset this esoteric yen, the Hoosier virus
manifests itself in sheer, downright roughneck enthusi-
asm—a la Al Terhune—over baseball, football, a rattling
good scrap in the ring, fishing, camping, barging about in
my launch, and my dog. You can criticize my stories, but I
warn you—lay off my launch or my dog!

As for fiction, I read over again, about once a year, such
stories as "Huckleberry Finn," "Treasure Island," "Septi-
mus," "The Virginian," "The Beloved Vagabond," and "Lord
Jim"—not to speak of Conrad's other works, and Kipling's
tales of the inimitable *Mulvaney*. And though I would like

very much to swank about as a two-fisted adventurer with the air—in addition—of a polished cosmopolite, I never get any further than first base. For—and there is nothing anomalous here!—as the editor swings a blue pencil over my stuff, so does Friend Wife edit me.

Best of luck to you... and I hope this will do.

Sincerely,

DON MCGREW.

www.ingramcontent.com/pod-product-compliance
Lightning Source LLC
Chambersburg PA
CBHW072353030726
47505CB00014B/1807